BROTHERS
OF THE RED SKY
SERIES

A HEALING Love

MARICCA WOOD

<u>**A HEALING LOVE:**</u>
Cover Design: Books and Moods
Editor: The Havoc Archives

*It's ok to hit rock bottom because the only direction
to go from there is up.*

Also By Maricca Wood

Desire Series
Desire's Curse
Desire's Blessing
Desire's End

Brothers of the Red Sky
A Healing Love

Note From The Author

This is the beginning of a four-book spin-off series of the Desire Series. These interconnected standalones will revolve around the four side characters who work for Hunter Gatlin, MMC in Desire's Blessing, at his private security firm, Red Sky Security. This book immediately picks up after the events of Desire's Blessing, book 2 in the Desire Series (interconnected standalone). Though this book can be read entirely on its own, it will contain spoilers about what transpires in Desire's Blessing and how our characters got to where they are now. If you don't want anything spoiled, I would suggest reading Desire's Blessing before continuing with this book.

-Enjoy

Playlist

Stronger by Mandisa

It Don't Hurt Like It Used To by Billy Currington

Voices In My Head by Falling In Reverse

Stamps by Cody Garrett

Love Story by Taylor Swift

Ladies And Gentlemen by Saliva

Brothers of Red Sky Security
CHARACTER DESCRIPTIONS

Call Sign: Boss

Origin of Call Sign: He's the owner of Red Sky Security

Real Name: Hunter Gatlin

Significant Other: Serenity (Renny) Jinx

Occupation: Ex-Navy SEAL, Owner of Red Sky Security.

Description: 29 years old, 6'3" with a physique built from years of military training wrapped in gorgeous, tanned skin, shoulder-length straight brown hair, full brown beard trimmed close to his face, scar bisecting left eyebrow, ice-blue eyes with a warm hazel center, a light dusting of chest hair, both arms covered in dark ink.

Vehicles: Blacked-out Harley Sportster, gunmetal grey Jeep Wrangler.

Call Sign: Sweeney

Origin of Call Sign: Because of his love for knives. He was named after the fictional serial killer from the mid-1800s, Sweeney Todd, who killed people with a straight razor.

Real Name: Grayson Rider

Significant Other: Addison (Addi) Thatcher

Occupation: Previously worked for Academi; a private military contracting company, and is now a bodyguard at Red Sky Security.

Description: 27 years old, 6'3" with sculpted muscles, short brown hair, golden eyes, sun-kissed skin, clean-shaven, square jawline, right arm painted with colorful ink.
Vehicles: Red and black Honda CBR motorcycle, Toyota Tacoma

Call Sign: Doc
Origin of Call Sign: He is a highly skilled sharpshooter and was named after the infamous gunslinger, Doc Holliday.
Real Name: Colt Rivers
Significant Other: N/A
Occupation: Did 4 years in the Army, then worked 4 years at Academi; a private military contracting company, and is now a bodyguard at Red Sky Security.
Description: 28 years old, 6'1", slim build with lean muscles, rich tawny skin, black hair cut short on top and faded in a medium fade on the sides, one arm is covered in dark ink and the other arm sports an old thin scar that runs vertically in a straight line on the outside of his forearm from elbow to wrist, wears a small silver cross earring in his left ear.
Vehicles: Red and black BMW S 1000 R motorcycle, black Dodge Ram.

Call Sign: Fuse
Origin of Call Sign: He's an explosives expert and pyro enthusiast.
Real Name: Logan Westgard
Significant Other: N/A

Occupation: Former Marine for 8 years, and is now a bodyguard for Red Sky Security.

Description: 29 years old, 6', chiseled physique, lightly tanned skin, sides of his head are shaved, and the blond hair on top is braided back and hangs to his shoulders, arctic eyes, reddish-brown beard trimmed close to his face.

Vehicles: Blue and black Harley Street Bob 114, red and black Chevy Camero.

Call Sign: Einstein

Origin of Call Sign: He's a brilliant tech wizard, skilled hacker, and avid video gamer.

Real Name: Levi Hardy

Significant Other: N/A

Occupation: Tech genius and hacker. Works behind the scenes at Red Sky Security and is the men's eyes and ears while they are out on protection duties.

Description: 23 years old, 6', slender with lean muscles, creamy skin, shaggy black hair kept under a beanie, deep blue eyes, free of any tattoos and piercings, always has his fingernails painted.

Vehicles: Green and black Kawasaki Ninja H2, blue Honda HR-V

Prologue
ADDISON

My name is Addison Thatcher, and this is the story of how my life went from a magical fairytale to an utter nightmare in the span of a single day.

Literally, *one* fucking day.

I wish I were joking, but my ugly reality is a constant, unfortunate reminder of the shitty hand Fate dealt me. Whatever I did to deserve this eludes me.

What should've been the best day of my life, of any girl's life, turned into something straight from a Blumhouse horror film. It's the day every girl spends years of their childhood planning, from clipping out various pages from bridal magazines to creating their dream wedding board.

I should know. I was one of them.

Then Jack Maddlen waltzed into my life. A man for whom I quickly fell head over heels. A man I wanted to build a future and share my life with as much as the body needs a heart and the earth needs the sun. He was smart, funny, and not to mention, the most attractive man I've ever had the pleasure of touching.

Six feet packed with mouthwatering lean muscles, wavy brown hair that made you want to sink your fingers into it, and deep emerald eyes that could turn any woman on with just one look. Not to mention he was a defense attorney with a plush bank account. He was the entire package… or so I thought.

My rose-colored glasses must've been sewn onto my face, or else I would have seen the true demon that lay beneath his gorgeous exterior. The truth is, Jack never loved me. He only used me to get close to my best friend, Serenity Jinx. He said as much not even twenty-four hours after we were married. What a fucking dick.

He'd bought a property in Hawaii, had both Serenity and I kidnapped from the resort where we got married, and hired two hit men to kill me so he could collect the multi-million dollar life insurance policy he took out on me without my knowledge. He'd planned on living in that home with Serenity, the woman he truly loved.

I don't blame Serenity or hold a grudge against her for what happened. She loved Jack, but only as one loves a close friend or a member of one's family. She was the one to stop him, sending three bullets deep into his chest cavity where his heart should've been. And rightfully so. I don't hold it against her for killing him either. He deserved it and much more.

My only regret is that I didn't do it myself for what he did to me. To us. He had stalked and tormented Serenity in the weeks leading up to our wedding—so much that she was a paranoid and nervous wreck.

Boy, I sure do know how to pick 'em, huh? So where does this leave me? At twenty-four, I've been reduced to an emotionally shattered shell of my former self, with my trust in men *completely* broken, with no light at the end of the tunnel. A tunnel so dark that you couldn't see your hand in front of your face. A tunnel that claims thousands of victims each year, without remorse, by showing no mercy and sucking you in to drown you with depression, grief, and heartache.

Chapter 1
ADDISON

The drive to the lawyer's office from the airport was rather quick. I don't remember much though. I don't even remember much about the flight back from Hawaii. I couldn't even tell you what the inside of Hunter's company jet looked like or any conversations that were had.

I kept to myself, with my knees pulled to my chest, my arms wrapped securely around my legs, and my vision trained on the clouds beyond my window. I wished more than once that I could turn into one so I could simply float away, without a care in the world, forgetting all about my troubles and my obliterated heart.

I do recall Sweeney checking in on me every now and then. However, I didn't speak. I simply didn't want to. All I wanted was to crawl into bed in a pitch-black room and never leave. I nodded weakly in answer to his questions. Thankfully, everyone left me alone so I could further process the horrors of what happened just a few days ago.

Has it only been a matter of days? It feels like a lifetime ago. Jack and I would've been wrapping up our honeymoon right about now. I should've been exhausted from exploring the islands, sightseeing, having so much mind-blowing sex with my new husband, and glowing with a golden tan from all the time spent relaxing on the beach.

Instead, I'm broken and bruised, metaphorically and physically, both inside and out. My husband was a monster that crawled out of the deepest, darkest pit of hell. My husband… God, how could I have been so stupid? How did I not see the signs?

After having a few days to reflect, the signs were there. How overly friendly Jack was with Serenity. The look in his eyes anytime she was around, as if she hung the moon. How he clung to every word she said, as if she were the center of his universe. Fuck, I'm such a fool!

Again, I don't blame Serenity. Not one bit. She never crossed that line with Jack. She's my best friend, my sister from another mister, and I trust her with my life. She loved Jack, but not in the way he wished. Not in the way he so desperately wanted.

A blinding light stings my vision as the car door opens. I hadn't realized we'd reached our destination. Hell, I didn't even realize that we were no longer on the jet. Not until I focus my gaze on Sweeney, who now stands outside my door with an outstretched hand and a kind smile on his ruggedly handsome face.

"Do we have to do this right now?" I grimace.

My voice is hoarse from crying and screaming into my pillow the last few days. On second thought, screw the bed in a pitch-black room. I'll settle for nothing less than a cold, dark hole to crawl into and never leave.

"Unfortunately." He holds my gaze, his honey eyes shining bright in the sun, showing off breathtaking hues of yellow and brown. "But it will be over soon, and you can put this behind you too."

I let out an exhausted sigh because he's right. I unbuckle my seatbelt and reach for his hand. I don't remember buckling myself in. Sweeney must've done it when he sat in the back with me as we left the airport. He helps me out of the car and closes the door behind me.

Hunter holds the door open for us as Serenity, Sweeney, and I enter the attorney's office building. Mr. Stanley calling Serenity and asking to speak with her about Jack's last will and testament instead of me has a bad feeling settling deep in the pit of my stomach.

We pack into the confined elevator, and Hunter presses the button for the fifth floor. My broken heart aches as I take in my best friend clutching her boyfriend's muscular arm like it's her life support. I'm so thankful that she was at least blessed with one of the good ones.

She'd met Hunter a few weeks ago on a dating site called Desire when she was searching for a new date for my wedding. She'd broken up with her long-term boyfriend after he'd cheated on her, and she didn't want to spend the weekend at the resort alone. I suggested she use the dating site to try to find a replacement date.

And in walked Hunter Gatlin. A six-foot-three former Navy SEAL packed with bulky muscles, shoulder-length brown hair he keeps mostly tied in a knot on the back of his head, a full brown beard he keeps neatly groomed close to his face, and unique ice-blue eyes with a warm hazel center. Dark ink that's disturbed by occasional scars covers both arms before disappearing beneath a T-shirt that forms tightly around his broad shoulders.

After separating from the military, he started his own security company, Red Sky Security, which provides temporary security details to affluent clients.

Hunter leans down and places a gentle kiss atop Serenity's raven hair as he rubs soothing circles across her back, causing emotions to constrict my throat like a boa with its prey. But in a good way. I wrap my arms around my middle, wishing I could crawl into myself and disappear as the metal doors part and we step off the elevator.

The red-carpeted hallway quiets our footsteps as we pass wooden doors with frosted glass windows that lead to other offices. We come to a stop outside one with *Mr. Stanley* stenciled on the door in big black letters.

We file into the small waiting room where a middle-aged woman greets us from behind a mahogany desk. "Good afternoon. How can I help you?"

"My name is Serenity Jinx. I'm supposed to meet Mr. Stanley about the last will and testament for Jack Maddlen."

The receptionist smiles sweetly at us all. "Please, have a seat. I'll let him know you have arrived."

We turn and take a seat in black-padded armchairs. About five minutes later, a man in his sixties with thinning white hair and a chubby face walks through a thick wooden door across the waiting room.

"Ah, Ms. Jinx, please come on back."

Shock and confusion mar the old man's rounded features when all four of us stand and follow one behind the other through the door and into his office.

"I'm sorry. I don't have enough chairs for everyone, but please, make yourselves comfortable," he says kindly, pointing to a black leather couch off to the side.

Sweeney and I take a seat on the couch as Serenity and Hunter take a seat in the two chairs that sit opposite the large desk.

"Were you all friends of Jack's?" he asks politely as he rounds his desk and takes a seat in the large, black swiveling chair.

"Something like that." Hunter's deep voice is cryptic.

"I'm so sorry for your loss," Mr. Stanley begins as he withdraws a few papers from a manila envelope and clears his throat. "This should go relatively quickly. It appears, Ms. Jinx, that Jack left everything to you."

Blood roars in my ears and my stomach churns as the lawyer's words sink in, unknowingly delivering news that only serves to twist the metaphoric knife Jack stabbed into my heart even deeper. I didn't think it was possible, but the fresh wave of pain is undeniable.

Serenity opens her mouth but closes it again, unsure what to say.

"I'm sorry, could you repeat that?" Her words come out shaky.

"Jack left everything in his will to you, Ms. Jinx," he repeats with a kind smile on his face.

This can't be happening…

Serenity sits up straight in her chair. "Everything?"

"Yes, ma'am. It states his parents' house and all its possessions, his current house and all its possessions, the property he just purchased in Hawaii and all its possessions, his car, his life insurance money, and the entirety of his bank accounts."

Mr. Stanley pulls his head back up to peer at her and removes his reading glasses, setting them down atop the papers on his desk.

Serenity points toward me. "But why me? Addi was his wife."

I know by the look on my friend's face that my features must be as white as the papers the lawyer clutches in his wrinkled hands. It feels as if someone sucked all the oxygen from the room. I try to take deep breaths, but my lungs won't fill, forcing me to take multiple shallow breaths instead. I'm vaguely aware of Sweeney next to me, his strong hand rubbing soothing circles across my back, but my mind is elsewhere.

"I was informed that he had gotten married last week, but he made no change to his will after that. In fact, this will has been the same since his parents passed a few years ago, except for the addition of new assets," Mr. Stanley informs us while keeping his tone as gentle as possible.

Holy… hell…

He truly was obsessed with Renny… from the very fucking start…

Serenity puts her foot down and shakes her head in disgust. "I don't want it. Any of it. If anyone deserves that stuff, it's Addi."

"You have a few options if that's how you truly feel. Option one, you can sign everything over to Addison. That would involve a lot of paperwork to sign ownership over to someone else, and we would have to do it for everything he owned. So, that would take a while. Option two, you can sell what you don't want and give her the money. Or option three, you can keep it all. This is completely up to you."

Serenity turns toward me. Her mossy eyes soften with sympathy. Or is it pity? I can't tell the difference anymore, and frankly, I don't care.

"Addi, what do you want to do?"

I open my mouth, but no sound comes out, forcing me to close it. My clammy grip on the couch tightens, and I know that without looking, my knuckles are bleached. My breaths begin to come faster, and I feel as if a panic attack is on the horizon.

I can't do this… I can't do this…

Finally, I manage to pull myself together enough to speak a few sentences.

"I don't want any of it either. I want nothing that reminds me of that piece of shit." I drop my gaze to the carpet and apologize no louder than a shaky whisper. "Sorry about the language."

Mr. Stanley has done nothing wrong. He's just an innocent messenger that unknowingly delivered another sick piece of Jack's game to us, putting the icing on the "fuck you" cake he spent the entirety of our relationship baking. Years of my life up in smoke, with nothing to show for it but devastation and pain. So much damn pain...

I can't wait for all this to be done with and for everything to blow over. I just want to try and get back to some semblance of normalcy in a life without Jack. The thought is utterly terrifying and makes me physically ill to my stomach. I've been with Jack for years. I was even living with him. What does *normal* even look like now?

Home… How can I go home to a place I shared with a monster? A home where every room and every piece of furniture has some story that reminds me of him. I can't. It would be too much.

I can't… I can't breathe…

My lungs constrict further, causing my chest to rise and fall at an alarming rate. I feel as if the walls of this small office are closing in on me and escape seems impossible.

Get a hold of yourself! I won't let these panic attacks rule me. I refuse to let Jack have any more effect on me.

"Eyes on me, sweetheart," Sweeney whispers in a tone so low that I almost miss it.

My brown eyes snap to him as one of his hands comes up to gently cup my face.

If my panic attack hadn't stolen my breath, the sight before my eyes would have. Sweeney is just as tall and broad as Hunter, with sun-kissed skin and eyes like ambered whisky. His brown hair is cut short on the sides and just long enough on top to run your fingers through. His square jawline is free from hair, showing off his rugged, manly features. Colorful ink covers his right arm, disappearing beneath his T-shirt.

His face is an unreadable mask, but worry swirls in his gaze as he peers at me. His thick dark brows are pulled together as if the solution to helping me lies somewhere within my irises.

"He doesn't get to decide how you feel anymore. Don't give him back that power."

"I'm trying," I choke out as tears threaten to fall. "After everything he did, he had to get one last fuck you to me. I... I don't even want to go home because of him."

He's quiet for a moment, as if pondering something. His vision shifts between mine, unsure of which to focus on.

"Then you'll come home with me until you find a place that's all your own."

I open my mouth, but the words get clogged in my throat. I close it and my eyes as I try to collect myself. After a few deep breaths, I manage, "No, no. I can't. I don't want to impose—"

"It's not imposing if I offered first, and if we're being honest, it wasn't even an offer. You *will* come home with me. You *will* stay there until you get a place of your own. You *will* let me help you heal in any way I can."

His words are demanding, but his eyes plead with me, desperately begging me to let him help.

Should I? Jack has completely shattered my trust, but I know from Sweeney's actions alone that he's nothing like Jack. They aren't even in the same universe by comparison. I know he'll keep his promise to help me in any way he can. And though Sweeney flew to Hawaii to help aid Hunter in rescuing us, killing two men to protect and save me, so effortlessly like a human squashing an ant, I know that he'd never hurt me as Jack did. Physically or mentally.

But *living* with another man? So soon after everything that had happened? I know he wouldn't touch me or try to pressure me into anything I wasn't ready for. My husband just betrayed me the day after our wedding, for Christ's sake. A relationship, even one that's purely physical, is the furthest fucking thing from my mind. I know I can't handle that right now, no matter how handsome the man is. But can I be roommates with another man so soon?

On the other hand, I truly don't want to live alone. I feel that's the quickest way to slip into a dangerous depression. Maybe I can room with Serenity for a little while? However, she is technically homeless.

Her house had burned down over two weeks ago. Jack, no surprise there, offered up his childhood home to her until she found a new place to live. That sick bastard just wanted her as close to him as possible. Another huge flashing neon sign that I so blindly missed. He stalked her inside that house in the days leading up to our wedding.

With how close Serenity and Hunter have grown, she'll probably want to stay with him. And if those two are living together, the last thing I want is to intrude and have to listen to them having sex all the time.

So… stay with Sweeney or live alone? A friend to help me heal *does* sound pretty nice right now.

"Ok," I whisper, and the spark of joy that flashes through his golden eyes tells me I made the right decision.

I hope…

He smiles brightly before dropping his hand from my face and turning forward, still rubbing small circles across my back with his other. His simple touch grounds me long enough to make it through the rest of this uncomfortable meeting.

"Then your best bet would be to sell everything and put the money into an account until y'all decide what you want to do with it," Mr. Stanley offers.

"Let's do that then," Serenity agrees with a curt nod.

Mr. Stanley has her sign a few papers before we're finally free to go.

Chapter 2

ADDISON

The silence amongst us was heavy when we finally left the lawyer's office. No one spoke until we piled into Hunter's gunmetal-grey Jeep Wrangler. With a twist of his wrist, the engine roared to life, and rock music turned low filled the cabin as we buckled up.

With a heavy sigh, Serenity is the first to break the silence. She twists in the front passenger seat to peer back at me, concern marring her pointed features. "How are you doing, Addi?"

"Oh, just peachy." Sarcasm drips from my words as I try to plaster a fake smile across my tired face.

"Honey," Serenity says with a sigh, seeing through the mask to the truth that lies beneath like she always has with me.

I cut her off, not wanting to talk anymore. "I just want a hot bath and some sleep."

I don't think I can take any more pity. From anyone.

"Can do." Hunter peers over his shoulder at me with a genuine smile. "What's your address? I'll drop you off first."

Before I can answer, Sweeney speaks up from beside me. "She's staying with me."

Hunter arches a brow at his friend, silently communicating his question. His eyes shift to me before flicking back to Sweeney.

"Don't worry, Big Daddy." Sweeney gives him a wide smile. "It's just until she gets back on her feet."

Hunter shifts his ice-blue and hazel gaze back to me. "Are you ok with this?"

"Yes." I give him a weak nod. "I…" My voice cracks, so I quietly clear my throat and try again. "I can't go back to that house. There are too many memories…"

"You don't have to explain. I understand. You could stay with Angel and me if you want," Hunter offers.

I knew Serenity would want to stay with him after all this. A small smile tugs at the corner of my mouth. "And listen to you two have crazy hot sex every night? No, thanks."

Serenity blushes hard and tries to bury her face in her hands while Hunter chuckles softly to himself.

"How do you know what their sex is like?" Sweeney squints and wiggles his brows at me with a mischievous grin lightening up his face.

"Girls talk." I shrug a shoulder before continuing. "Plus, just look at him—all hot, muscular, and manly. He doesn't strike me as the soft and gentle type."

"Alright!" Serenity is now as red as an apple as she cuts the conversation from going any further. Hunter and Sweeney both roar with laughter. "If you're truly ok with this, we can drop y'all off and go pack up your things and bring them to you."

My aching heart swells with love for my sister. "You don't have to do that, Renny."

"It's no bother at all, I promise. I wouldn't want to go back there either if I were you. I got you, sis."

She shoots me a wink before turning back around and signaling for Hunter to start driving.

He must know where to go because he drives without turning on the GPS. It would make sense though. Sweeney has worked with him for years now. I'm sure they've been over to each other's houses numerous times over the years.

Twenty minutes later, we pull into a small neighborhood with beautiful two-story duplexes. The houses couldn't be more than ten years old, each covered with brick, wood, or a combination of both. Each home is equipped with a two-car garage with beautiful flower beds lining the front walkways.

I can't help but gape in awe. I didn't know what to expect when it came to the type of home Sweeney would live in, but this caught me by surprise. We pass a handful of duplexes before Hunter pulls into the left driveway of a stunning house. It's built of beautiful grey brick halfway up, then dark blue-painted wood the rest of the way, topped with a black shingled roof.

Sweeney jumps out and rounds the back of the Jeep as he begins to unload our luggage. I climb out and try to school my features from a mixture of shock and admiration.

Serenity rolls her window down and peers over at me. "We'll be back in about an hour or two with your things, ok?"

I turn to her. "Thank you." I shift my gaze toward Hunter. "Both of you."

He nods in return.

I round the front of the Jeep where Sweeney is waiting for me with my luggage in one hand and his black duffle bag slung over a broad shoulder. I don't miss the way his muscles bulge and flex with each movement.

"You look surprised." He's sporting a cocky grin as Hunter backs out of the driveway and drives off down the road.

I follow him up the three steps onto his covered front porch and wait as he sets my suitcase down and digs his keys out of his jeans pocket.

"I just didn't peg you for the suburban, HOA type."

"You can peg me anytime you like." He gives me a playful wink before unlocking his front door and stepping aside, motioning for me to enter first.

"Don't tempt me. I might be into that," I shoot back, and don't miss the shock that enters his eyes as I step over the threshold.

He throws his head back with laughter as he shuts the door and locks it, setting our bags down in the small foyer. The space is cozy with a small closet nestled in the left corner and a door to the right that I'm guessing leads to the garage. The walls are painted a soft cream with white baseboards and elegant crown molding. Light hardwood floors run vertically from the front of the house to the back, making the space appear more open.

His keys clink against a small glass bowl that sits on a wooden entry table positioned to the left that contains… photographs?

"A suburban home *and* you set out pictures. Who are you?" I tease as I skim over the five-by-sevens resting in thick, dark wood frames.

One is of Sweeney and a young woman dressed in a black graduation robe with a gold sash draped around her neck. *Valedictorian* is stamped into the sash in black font. He has his arm wrapped around the woman's neck as he pulls her to his side, about to give her a knuckle sandwich.

I take a guess. "Is this your sister?"

They have the same shade of brown hair, though hers falls in luscious waterfall curls that cascade down her shoulders, and they share the same golden eyes. Their smiles are almost identical too. The sight brings the ghost of a smile to my face. A rare occasion this week.

"Yeah. That's Sophie." Love fills his voice. "That was taken last year when she graduated college."

"I see she got all the beauty in the family."

He snorts and I shift my gaze to the next one. A group photo with the men he works with. Sweeney, Hunter, Fuse, Doc, and Einstein are gathered around a bonfire, all with a beer raised in salute and smiles brightening their faces.

I think back to the day I met them all. Serenity had asked if I wanted to join them for a few beers. I was more than happy to get out of the house for a while. Jack had been working late all week, making sure he was caught up on all his case files so he could pass them off to a coworker while he was on leave for our wedding and honeymoon.

My mouth sours as if I swallowed acid, and I clench my jaw to keep the nausea down. He wasn't working late… Not every day, at least. It was his excuse so he could stalk Serenity freely.

I close my eyes, take a slow, deep breath, and release it even more slowly, clearing my mind of all things Jack-related. I open them and land back on the picture of Sweeney and his friends. I'm not afraid to admit, I was a bit scared when I first met them. They looked rather intimidating. All were either ex-military or worked with government private contractors. You know the type. I try to remember the story they told me behind each of their call signs, but I can't remember the exact details.

I turn back and start down the hallway that leads to the rest of the home. I don't have to turn around to know Sweeney is following close behind. Though his steps are silent, I can feel his dominating presence. We pass a small half-bathroom to the left and a carpeted staircase on the right that leads to the second floor.

The back half opens before me. A large living room, dining room, and kitchen are all open and connected. An entertainer's dream. More photos and artwork adorn the walls, and the light from the numerous large windows brightens the space fully without the need for artificial light.

I turn and make my way up the stairs, fully aware of my new roommates' gaze on me the entire way. I observe more photos hanging along the walls of the stairwell. A small loft at the top of the stairs is filled with bookshelves and a cozy lounge chair.

I point to the door on my left. "Bedroom?"

"My room, yes." I turn right to head down another hallway. "Your bathroom." He points to the left.

I let out a small teasing sigh. "I guess it will do."

He snorts and points to the right. "Laundry room, and two bedrooms." He motions to the doors in front of me. "Take your pick."

I point to the one on the right. "Does this one share a wall with your bathroom?"

"Yes."

I step toward the room on the left. "I'll take this one then."

"Too tempting to picture me when you hear me shower?" he teases.

"Not at all. I just don't care to hear you jerking off in there," I throw back as I enter my new bedroom.

The farthest one away from him as possible. The room is simple. A queen-sized bed with a large, slatted, wooden headboard, a nightstand, and a dresser all in a matching dark walnut color. A simple powder-blue bedspread covers the bed with matching throw pillows and drapes.

I can't help but turn around and cross my arms over my chest. My breath hitches when I see him leaning against the doorframe, hands tucked into the pockets of his jeans. His gaze is locked on me as I take in the space, and my aching heart nearly skips a beat.

I clear my throat of any emotions before I speak. "Does a woman live here with you?"

He hikes a brow in amusement. "Why do you ask?"

"You didn't answer my question," I push back, raising a brow of my own.

He shrugs his shoulders. "If one did, would it matter?"

"Um… Yeah, it would. One, it would be awkward. Very awkward. And two, that's the reason I didn't stay with Hunter and Renny. The last thing I want is to hear two people having sex often."

I push away the ping of jealousy that tries to surface. I barely know the man, and I just got out of a horrible relationship. Dating or sleeping with someone is literally the furthest thing from my mind. Even though my heart has been shattered, my body still reacts on its own when in the presence of beauty. Or in Sweeney's case, a goddamn masterpiece. Good to know my hormones still work, for way in the future when I'm ready to date again. Though that thought is enough to churn my empty stomach.

"Is someone jealous?" he teases with a smile.

"I barely know you. Why would I be jealous?"

I ignore the rational part of my brain that tries to scold myself for agreeing to stay in a house with a complete stranger. *Smart move, Addi.*

He removes his hands from his pockets and crosses them over his chest. "Why all the sudden questions?"

I place my fists on my hips and pin him with a glare. "Why are you avoiding answering them?"

"I can see living with you is going to be fun." His grin is full of mischief.

"I won't be living here if someone else lives here with you," I correct.

"Sorry, no take-backsies. And to put your cute little mind at ease, I live alone. Minus Sharleen." My brows pull together, and he explains. "She's a harmless old lady whose spirit lingers here. That's why I have that reading nook. I've found her lounging there too many times to count."

My jaw drops in shock, and I try not to be obvious as I peer around his large frame and down the hallway. "Please tell me you're joking."

A wicked grin and a shrug of his broad shoulders is his only response.

I take a deep breath and try again. "Have you ever lived with a woman?"

"No, sweetheart." He pushes off the doorframe and takes a step toward me. "Why?"

I ignore the way my body tries to wake up when it senses his closeness. "Because this home was definitely furnished and designed by a woman."

"How do you know it wasn't me?"

I motion behind me with my hand. "Because no straight man would ever bother matching the color of the bedspread to the drapes."

He takes another step. "Very observant of you. Do you like it?"

"Your home is beautiful," I answer honestly.

"I'll be sure to relay your compliments to Sophie." He gives me a wink and stops a few feet away.

His sister. I nod in realization and try not to sigh in relief that no other woman lives here.

I take a breath and square my shoulders. "Any rules I should know about, going forward?"

"Like what?" He cocks his head to the side, and I groan inwardly.

"Like Thursday nights are poker with the boys, so I'll need to make myself scarce. The second shelf in the fridge is yours. Sunday nights are for orgies."

Sweeney's laughter echoes off the bedroom walls, the sound scooping the pieces of my broken heart into a neat little pile as if they could be reconstructed. "First, orgy nights are on Fridays. You can't do something like that on the Lord's day. That's just wrong. Second, I keep my snacks in a private stash, hidden away, so feel free to eat anything in the kitchen. And third, even if I have the boys over, this is your home now just as much as it's mine. I will never make you leave for any reason."

I snort at his first two conditions, finding myself thankful for his wonderful sense of humor. But his third condition settles over me like a security blanket I don't realize I need at this moment.

"Thank you." I let my arms fall to my sides as I begin to pick at the hem of my shirt. "For letting me stay here. I promise I won't be a pain in your ass. And I'm more than happy to split the bills with you until I find my own place."

"As long as it's an enjoyable pain, then we're good." He smiles before his features turn more serious. "You won't pay me a penny. And if you do, I'll put it aside in an envelope for you to use for a new place if you move out."

"We'll see." I purposefully don't let myself linger on the fact that he said *if* I move out, not *when* I move out.

"We will." He chuckles. "Now, get cleaned up and get some rest."

"I don't have anything to change into. Nothing clean, at least. I need to do laundry from… the trip." My voice weakens as the memory of this week settles back over me.

Without a word, Sweeney turns on his heels and disappears down the hallway. I stand there confused, and can't stop my gaze from sliding to the reading nook at the end of the hallway. He better've been joking when he mentioned he had a ghost living here. I swallow audibly and pray that if Sharleen is in fact real, she's a gentle old soul who'll leave me alone.

My eyes dart around my room as quick fear causes goosebumps to sprout up my arms. I hope she's not in the room with me now, watching me. A chill rolls down my spine, and I quickly force her out of my mind as Sweeney returns a minute later with a black T-shirt and a pair of boxers clutched in his large hand.

"You can wear these."

"So, you're a boxers guy?" I snort as I accept the clothes from him and drop my gaze to the carpeted floor. "Thank you."

"Anytime, sweetheart." He turns, heads back downstairs, and leaves me all alone.

Chapter 3

SWEENEY

I guess the saying about how you never stop learning new things about yourself is true because, apparently, I'm a glutton for punishment. What the hell have I gotten myself into? Offering for Addi to stay here is a recipe for disaster. But I couldn't sit back and do nothing while she fell apart. She didn't want to go back to her house, and I don't blame her. I wouldn't either. And she had no other place to go.

I tried to convince myself that she could get her own place. Maybe that would be good for her, but I know better. Someone who just went through something as traumatic as she and Serenity did should not be left alone. At least not for a while. They have a treacherous darkness threatening to drag them down to the darkest, deepest pits of hell, and they need someone to tie them to the light. To keep them from slipping into a nasty depression.

I run my fingers through my hair, tugging lightly at the strands as I descend the stairs. I relish the slight sting of my scalp as I kick off my boots and place them in the hall closet, retrieve our bags, and make my way back upstairs. The door to the spare bathroom is closed, and a soft yellow light illuminates from beneath.

I groan as the sound of the shower fills my ears and I force my brain not to imagine the goddess standing naked beneath the hot sprays. I was never one to believe in love at first sight, but with God as my witness, I fell for her like a damn fool the moment I saw her in that bar before they left for her wedding.

But hell, she looked so beautiful in that little blue sundress. Actually, beautiful doesn't even come close to describing her. Celestial is the closest thing I can think of, and even that seems like an understatement. The way the thin material hugged her curves and showed off a teasing amount of those thick and sexy legs of hers should've been illegal. I was half tempted to find the dress designer just so I could send them a thank-you card.

I will never admit how many times I envisioned those legs wrapped around my head as I took my cock in my hand and worked myself till I spilled in the shower. The moment I learned she was getting married, a part of me died, but that didn't stop me from admiring her from afar.

The day they left for Hawaii, I drank my feelings away as I sat on my couch and tried to lose myself in the sports channel. I woke up the next day and moped around the house like a lovesick puppy. Pathetic, I know. And don't get me started about how I felt the day of her wedding.

The boys must've felt my suffering because Einstein called and said everyone was meeting in his office to watch some football. Apparently, the little evil genius hacker was able to get the NFL package for free. I was beyond thankful for the distraction my brothers provided me with. But when we got the phone call from Boss that he couldn't find Serenity, a bad feeling settled deep in my stomach.

I couldn't get to that airport fast enough, and I know the pilot considered throwing me from the plane mid-flight if I asked him if he could go any faster one more time. Once Einstein got us a location on Jack and the women, Boss broke numerous traffic laws to get us there quickly.

What little control I had over my rage was hanging on by a single thread as I was forced to watch two criminals covered in trashy ink throw Addi into the trunk of their car. When Boss gave me the green light to go after them, a wicked grin spread across my face, and my hands twitched with the need to carve them up with my knives.

I had followed behind them and pride blossomed through me when I saw Addi burst from that trunk and take off into those woods. I knew that woman had fire in her spirit. I knew she'd never go down without a fight. Killing both those criminals pleased me in ways that would have me admitted to a psych ward if a therapist ever learned it. Once I had Addi safe and in my arms, only then could I finally begin to breathe normally.

After placing her luggage inside her room, I approach the small laundry closet in the hall. I unzip my duffle bag and pile everything into the washing machine, not bothering to separate clothes from socks and underwear. Why waste more water and detergent by running multiple loads? They all get washed the same. I toss in a detergent pod, close the lid, and start the machine. I'm so thankful I splurged on an endless hot water tank as I enter my bedroom and close the door behind me. I cross the room and enter my bathroom, peel the clothes from my body, and toss them into the hamper that rests inside my closet.

After starting the shower, I step into the spray, not bothering to wait for the water to heat up first. A hiss escapes my lips as the cold hits my heated body, hoping it will quell the urge to climb into my new roommate's shower so I can help her wash all those hard-to-reach spots.

Shit… I run my hands over my face. So much for ridding my brain of those dirty thoughts. The water begins to warm, and I groan as I take my hardened member in my hand. I close my eyes and let my head fall back as I begin to tug slowly along my throbbing shaft.

What would she think if she found out I was touching myself to the thought of her in the shower, not fifty feet from me? I'll be a good boy and keep my hands to myself. I may tease and taunt her with my words, but I won't touch her until she's ready and begs for it. Until then, my hand and my fantasies will have to do.

What if she was touching herself too? *No, you idiot*… Sex is the furthest thing from her mind after everything that happened. Of course, she's not touching herself. *But*… *What if*… I allow myself to visualize what she would look like. What she would sound like.

Her long brown hair soaked and clinging to her body. Her head tipped back in pleasure as she angled the showerhead so the spray hit that little spot that would send her over the edge. Would she use her fingers too? Pumping them inside herself as the water pressure worked her clit. Would she grab a handful of those beautiful tits? So full, inviting, and fucking perfect.

I tug myself faster as I focus on what her moans would sound like. Small, little breathy sounds that I know would drive me completely feral. The sounds would echo off the tile walls like the most beautiful symphony. I feel my orgasm fast approaching as I place a hand against the shower wall for support and quicken my pace.

Addi seems like a screamer. *Fuck…* I groan. What I wouldn't give to know if that were true. All too soon, my balls draw in close to my body, and I grunt as I empty myself. My cum shoots to the shower floor and washes down the drain, and I don't stop tugging until I've emptied myself.

I stay like that, panting, to catch my breath for a moment longer before I straighten. I quickly run through soaping up my body and hair before rinsing myself clean and stepping out of the shower. I towel off, throw on a pair of boxers, and slip into a pair of black pajama pants and a dark green T-shirt.

As I leave my room, the sounds of Addi's shower still running are enough to make me groan aloud. I quickly descend the stairs before my twitching hand takes on a mind of its own and opens that bathroom door. Even though I've just come, my body's ready to do it again because it wasn't in the way it so desperately wanted to.

I'm halfway through making dinner, stirring the pasta noodles in a pot of boiling water, when the sound of bare feet padding down the hallway gains my attention. I peer up, only to have a minor heart attack. Addi strides into the space, wearing nothing but my T-shirt and boxers.

She has not a lick of makeup on, and her freshly brushed brown and blonde damp strands have been left down to dry. Even though the bruising on her cheek and her split lip are mostly healed, wounds she'd acquired while battling through hell on that island, she's still the most beautiful woman I've ever seen. The sight of her so bare and comfy in my home has my dick throbbing and my pulse racing.

Living with her will be fun indeed, I quote myself from our earlier conversation, and sigh inwardly. I turn back around and stir the noodles again, scooping one up and blowing on it a few times before eating it, testing to see if they are done or need longer to cook.

A few more minutes, I decide, as I set the spoon down and turn toward my new roommate, who climbed atop a barstool and is now watching me. Thank God there's a four-foot island separating us right now.

She hikes a brow at me. "You cook too?"

My mind momentarily takes me back to my childhood and all the evenings I spent in the kitchen with my mom and little sister. She taught us everything we know. I'm no chef, but I can confidently prepare somewhat complex meals that won't leave the consumers at risk of eating charred food or suffering a horrible case of food poisoning.

"It was either learn how to cook or eat out every night, and since I'm watching my figure, I chose the former." I smile and she rolls her eyes at me.

What a little brat. I'd like to… Nope! Uh-uh! Stop that line of thought right now.

"You're an enigma, you know that?"

She smiles at me, but it's small and shaky. Fuck, I wish I could see her true smile again. Like I did that day when I first laid eyes on her. She was so full of life, funny, and such a smartass. I don't care how long it takes—weeks, months, fucking years—I'll help her get back to that and see it again.

"I can't be predictable. It makes me an easy target. Gotta keep my enemies on their toes." I walk over to the fridge and hold up a glass bottle. "Beer?"

"If that's the strongest alcohol you have, I'll take it."

I laugh, pop the top, and slide it across the white marble counter, careful to keep my hands to myself. I'm nowhere near trustworthy enough right now to resist exploring that supple body of hers if I touch it. Even by accident.

Addi takes a long swig of her beer, and I open one for myself. "I have hard liquor, but I feel we need to work up to that. Baby steps, sweetheart."

She rolls her eyes again and takes another drink. My grip tightens around my beer ever so slightly at the defiance, but I take a deep breath and push it away.

"So, what's for dinner?"

"Mac and cheese."

Addi nearly chokes on her drink, coughing a few times before furrowing her brows. "What are you, ten years old?"

I stir and test the noodles again. "What's wrong with macaroni and cheese?"

I remove the pot from the stove, turn off the burner, and pour everything into a strainer I have waiting in the sink.

"Nothing, it's just… Dude, you're giving me whiplash." She sighs, but a hint of an honest smile shows through, and damn if it doesn't spark warmth in my cold heart.

"Like I said, gotta keep 'em guessing," I say over my shoulder and shake any remaining water from the noodles.

I place them in a large bowl as well as a pan of hamburger meat I cooked up earlier. I remove the cheese from a small saucepan that was simmering on low heat, so it didn't burn, and add it to the mixture. After mixing and making sure everything is coated evenly in the cheese sauce, I dump the bowl into a rectangular casserole dish.

After setting it aside, I turn back toward Addi, who's watching me intently. Holding up a Ziploc bag of croutons, I question, "Fist or tenderizer?"

She stares at me like I've grown a second head. "You've lost me."

"They need to be crushed for the topping. Do you want to use your fist or a meat tenderizer?"

She's quiet for a moment, and my eyes track the way she bites the inside of her cheek when she's lost in thought. I shift my gaze up in time for her to answer, "Tenderizer."

"Good choice." I grab the tool from a cylindrical utensil container resting atop my counter and hand both over to her.

She wastes no time in pulverizing the croutons into tiny pieces, most likely visualizing that it's Jack's face she's hitting. She goes on a little longer than necessary, but I don't comment, knowing she needs to let out some of her frustration and hurt any way she can.

I take another drink of my beer, pretending that I didn't see the single tear that has betrayed her by falling. She quickly swipes it away, and red-hot anger builds within. Anger toward a man who promised to love and protect this woman's heart, mind, and soul, only to brutally obliterate them instead. My jaw clenches so tightly that it hurts, but after numerous slow and steady breaths, I feel my rage start to dissipate.

When she's had her fill, she hands them back to me. I sprinkle shredded cheese over the top of the casserole, sprinkle the crushed croutons, and place the dish in the oven for about ten minutes. Only long enough to melt the cheese on top. A stomach growls, and my eyes drift toward Addi, whose face now has a sexy, rosy blush creeping across it.

"Fuck me…" The words are dragged out as I groan quietly. "It's almost done." I chuckle. "When was the last time you ate?"

She didn't eat on the plane, and she's been with me ever since, so breakfast had to be the last time. No wonder her stomach is growling.

"I'm not sure." Her voice is so small that even a mouse would be impressed.

I completely freeze from my task of dishes, and slowly pivot toward her, all amusement gone as I pin her with a look. "What the fuck do you mean, you don't know?" She doesn't answer. Rather, she drops her gaze to the counter as she pretends to swipe at invisible crumbs. "Eyes on me, sweetheart." I snap my fingers, causing her vision to quickly jump to mine again. "How long has it been since you last ate, Addison?"

The sound of me using her full name causes her to flinch. Rightfully so. If she hasn't been taking care of herself, I swear I'll bend her over my knee and smack her round ass till she promises to eat at least three square meals a day. *No, you won't do that, because that would be* highly *inappropriate,* I warn myself. But I'll find some other way to punish her, so she learns her lesson.

She sighs and her shoulders slump in defeat. "When we all met for dinner at the small diner in the resort."

"The diner?" I try to recall the memory. "That was two days ago! You barely picked at your food then and you haven't eaten since? Jesus, how are you walking around and functioning right now?"

I'm seeing red again, but I'm trying not to take it out on her. I know she's been through a lot.

"I haven't had much of an appetite since..." Her voice cuts off as if she knows she's in trouble.

"I. Don't. Care," I grit out before I take a calming breath. "Your body needs fuel. I understand you went through something very traumatic. Trust me, I'm no stranger to trauma, but that's no excuse to stop taking care of yourself."

"I know." She finally looks up at me. "I just..." A heavy sigh escapes her lips. "It's just another thing added to my list of things to work on."

"Well, you don't have to tackle that list alone. I'm here to help with it all."

The timer beeps. I remove the dish from the oven and rest it atop the stove to cool. I finish washing the last little bit of dishes, and by the time I'm done, the food is ready to eat. I grab us both an extra-large helping. For her because her body needs the calories even though her stomach's probably shrunk to half its usual size by now, and for me because I'm a large man. My body takes a lot of calories to function properly.

I slide her the bowl and wait in anticipation as she takes a cautious bite and then closes her eyes and fucking *moans*. The grip on my bowl tightens to a dangerous level that risks shattering the ceramic if I don't ease up.

"Good?" I ask through gritted teeth, willing my groin to stop growing.

"This is the best mac and cheese I've ever had!" She scoops a large spoonful and piles it in her mouth.

I chuckle but look away, so I don't begin imagining that pretty mouth of hers being filled with other things. Things that I'm quite positive would also gain a moan like that one. Things I have absolutely no right to be thinking of right now.

Chapter 4
ADDISON

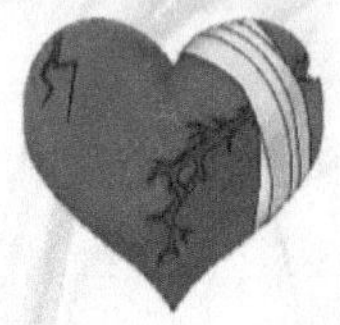

I may have given him crap about making macaroni and cheese for dinner, but it was so good, I had a second bowl. Even though I'm bloated as hell, I regret nothing. Not a single, cheesy, delicious noodle. Now, we're curled up on his large sectional couch with fresh beers and enough space to seat two people between us.

Sweeney has an old football game playing on the TV as background noise. He asked what I wanted to watch, but I didn't want to admit that a guilty pleasure of mine has always been trashy reality dating shows. Mainly because the last time I watched that with a man, it was with… Well, we won't speak his name, but you know who. I don't know if I can ever watch those things again.

Though sports take a close second. Some of the fondest memories from my childhood involved me and my father curling up on the couch, stuffing our faces with greasy pizza as we cheered on our favorite teams. I let out a small sigh, and I can feel his gaze on me, but I keep my vision forward. I'm thankful for the space. Lord knows I need it right now. And I'm grateful that he stays close enough that I don't feel entirely alone. I open my mouth to voice that, but the doorbell nearly sends me jumping off the couch in fright.

"Someone's skittish." Sweeney chuckles and removes his phone from the pocket of his pajama bottoms.

He must've pulled up the security feed because, with a press of a button, he speaks into his phone. "Hey, Big Daddy. Renny, come on in."

I remove the blanket from my lap, set my beer down, and stand to greet Hunter and Serenity as they enter. They're in comfy clothes too, having the same idea we had about getting cleaned up after a long flight. Serenity briefly acknowledges Sweeney before throwing her arms around me and squeezing tightly as if I'll vanish if she doesn't.

I return the intensity of the hug, craving the connection with my best friend.

She pulls away, her mossy vision scanning me over before she arches a brow after observing me in a man's shirt and boxers. "How are you doing?"

A half-hysterical laugh slips out. "I know you mean well, but I'm so tired of being asked that question."

"Got it! Don't ask anymore. Can do." She smiles at me and then lets her gaze roam over the space. "This is not what I pictured Sweeney's house looking like. Does he live with someone?"

I smile inwardly, loving how she picked up on the same decorating question I had. Both Hunter and Sweeney have gone out front, presumably to start bringing in my things. As if right on cue, both men walk through the door, each with a large bag or suitcase in tow.

"I thought the same thing. Apparently, Sophie, his younger sister, decorated the place."

She cracks a smile and nudges me with her elbow. "Maybe I should have her do Hunter's place too."

The men descend the stairs and exit the home again before coming in with another armload of bags.

"Don't worry." Serenity follows my gaze. "I got everything you asked for. Every stitch of clothing you own, all your bathroom products, everything from your nightstand, your phone charger, and your favorite coffee mugs."

"Thank you." I let out a sigh, feeling a huge weight lift from my shoulders.

"Also, I drove your car here." She places the keys in my hand. "It's now in the driveway."

"I'm sorry I asked you to—"

"Don't you dare!" She stops me with a raised finger like a mother to her child. "You have every right to never want to step foot in that house again, and no one would hold it against you. I'm fine, Addi. I promise. It was weird, but it wasn't hard for me. Not like it would've been for you."

Her smile is kind and her eyes are gentle as she places a hand on my arm. "I also packed something special for you. Small pink suitcase, inside pocket." She shoots me a wink and then whispers, "You're welcome."

"You're horrible!"

I shake my head but give her a genuine smile that feels foreign nowadays. Her green eyes practically glow at the sight. God, it feels as if it's been years since my lips have turned up toward the sky rather than down toward the ground.

"Unless…" Serenity wiggles her brows suggestively and motions her eyes towards Sweeney, who has just descended the stairs again.

"Absolutely not!" I whisper, and feel a blush beginning to paint my cheeks. "Not happening."

Thankfully, the conversation is halted before she can say something that would have my cheeks blazing. A sign that would easily convey our topic of discussion as Hunter and Sweeney enter the living room and stop next to us. The thought of involving myself with another man is enough to quicken my breath, send anxiety prickling my skin, and turn my palms clammy.

I've never been one to have casual hookups. I've always needed some level of trust when it came to the guys I involved myself with, but my ex took that trust and shattered it into millions of microscopic pieces. My shoulders deflate as I let out a long, quiet exhale.

I pray that *eventually,* I'll be whole enough to enter a relationship again, but that will be years down the road. At least. I swear, if You Know Who ruined me for any future relationship with a man, I'll summon him and attach his spirit to an elevator, so he'll be forced to listen to that horrible, ear-bleeding instrumental music for all eternity.

"Hey." Hunter grins, most likely noticing my blush and wondering what we were just talking about. From what I know about him, he's freakishly observant of his surroundings. "How are you—"

"Nope! Zip it, baby." Serenity cuts him off and bites her lips, trying not to smile.

Hunter tugs his dark brows together and peers at me, expertly observing me with his trained vision. "Never mind." He draws out the words cautiously and clears his throat before continuing. "We've got all your stuff unloaded and brought up to your room."

I shift my gaze between my best friend and her boyfriend. "Thank you, again. I truly appreciate the both of you."

"Do y'all want to stay for a drink?" Sweeney offers.

"Nah, it's getting late and this one needs rest." Hunter nods toward Serenity. "If you need anything, don't hesitate to reach out."

"I will." I nod toward him, and my next words fall out of my mouth in an awkward rush before I can stop them. "Meaning I'll reach out, not that I'll hesitate."

Hunter chuckles and extends a hand toward Serenity. "I know what you meant."

"Talk to you soon." She places a soft kiss on my cheek, gives me a quick hug, and takes her boyfriend's hand as they exit the home and close the door behind them.

Sweeney locks and sets the alarm before returning. "It is getting late. You should get some rest too. Don't worry about unpacking. I can help you with it in the morning if you'd like."

"It's ok. It's not that much, really. And I'm looking forward to the busy work." It will help distract my brain from reliving everything with my ex. I turn and start heading toward the stairs. "Good night, Sweeney."

"Grayson." His deep voice halts my steps as I turn and peer up at him, my face scrunched with curiosity. "That's my name. Grayson Rider. You don't have to keep calling me Sweeney."

An odd sensation shoots through my numb chest. If I had to guess, it felt almost like… warmth. "Good night, Grayson."

After testing out the name, I find it fitting. Nice.

I don't miss the slight widening of his eyes and the tick of his jaw before he masks his features and gives a sly grin and a wink. "Good night, sweetheart."

I turn and make my way up the stairs to my new room. Bags and suitcases varying in size and color are sitting in the corner of the space. I take a deep breath, pull the first one into the middle of the room, unzip it, and get to work, craving the busyness and the distraction this will bless my brain with. If only for a few minutes.

I hear Sweeney—sorry, Grayson's—door close twenty minutes into my unpacking. After another hour, I place the last bit of clothes in a dresser drawer and place the bag on the floor of the closet with the others. I laughed to myself when I found the hidden item Serenity had packed for me, saying I would thank her later. It and its charger are now safely tucked away in the bottom drawer of my dresser, hidden under a few layers of clothes.

I don't know how long it will be before I bust out that toy, or if I can even use it with Grayson being just down the hall. I wonder if he'll get himself off while I'm in the house, or will he wait until he's alone? Though I'm sure he has a girlfriend or at least a list of willing women he could call up when he feels the need.

He doesn't strike me as someone who'd jerk off when they can have any woman he wants just from his looks alone. A pang of jealousy tries to take root deep within, but I yank it up, stomp on the plant, set it on fire, and kick the ashes away before it can cause any damage.

I agree, that was probably overkill, but I take no chances with that emotion. Jealousy is an ugly bitch, and I'm dealing with too much at the moment to pile that on top of everything else. He's not mine. I'm not his. I'm not in *any* position to be anyone's right now, not with all the mental and emotional healing I've been forced to rebuild from scratch.

After I plug my phone charger in and rest it atop my nightstand, I plop down on my bed and blow out a long, slow exhale. This is going to be my new home for the foreseeable future. At least it's a nice and comfortable one. With a ghost of a smile on my face, I throw back the covers and slide beneath, snuggling deep into the waiting warmth.

With a tire iron in hand, I'm ready. I know that the moment I pull that release, if it works, the kidnappers will be notified and stop. I'll have a small window in which to make my escape.

I take a deep breath and pull the trunk release. To my surprise, it pops open. The driver slams on the brakes, causing me to roll to the back of the trunk from the force of the sudden stop. Before the car can come to a complete halt, I leap from the trunk and sprint off into the woods.

"Hey! Get the fuck back here!" T, one of the criminals Jack hired to kill me, yells as he leaps from the car and sprints after me.

I don't have to look back to know that both men are now chasing me. I have to focus on where I'm going. I duck under low branches, weave through the trees, and vault over fallen logs, knowing that if I spare a glance backward, I could trip, and the chase would be over.

Both men shout vulgar language at me and threaten to shoot, but I don't slow my pace. I'll be dead if I do. This is my only chance at survival. The threat of them behind me motivates me to move faster than I thought possible, but not fast enough. The force of what feels like a linebacker slams into me, tackling me to the forest floor. I swing the tire iron with all my might and knock T on the side of the head.

"Ah! You fucking bitch!" T shouts as he rolls off me a few feet away, holding the side of his bony face. His black hair is buzzed close to his scalp, and his pale skin is covered in cheap chicken scratch ink.

I don't spare him a second glance as I quickly get to my feet and take off running again. T catches up to me a second time, knocking me to the ground, but he's ready this time. When I swing the tire iron at him, he catches it with his hand and rips it from my grasp, tossing it to the side.

He rolls me to my back, straddles me, and sends a bony fist flying into the left side of my face. I cry out in pain as a second and third punch land back to back.

"Doesn't feel good when someone hits you, does it?" he spits at me.

I'm dazed as Baldy finally catches up to us. Much like T, he's covered in ink, including his meaty neck and face.

"Well, I guess here is as good of a place as any. I doubt we'll be able to get her back to the car unnoticed," Baldy says in his scratchy voice, his black, soulless eyes boring into me.

"Hold her wrists down," T instructs his partner. The large man grabs my limp wrists, places them above my head, and kneels onto my palms, using his weight to pin them in place. I grunt from the pain, still dazed. "I don't know about you, but I want to have a little fun with this one first before we kill her."

"Burn in hell!" I spit a mouthful of blood at T, who still straddles my thighs.

"Tell me something I don't know, sweetheart. But until then, I'll relish in the joys of the living." T rips the front of my tank top down to my navel, exposing the dark purple lace push-up bra that plumps up my already voluptuous cleavage. "Fuck, girl! God definitely blessed you."

T places his slender, bony hands over each breast, giving them a good squeeze as he lets out a groan of pleasure. I try to turn myself from side to side, try bucking my hips to get him off me, but I'm held tightly in place.

T's voice is laced with hunger as he says, "Let's find out if you're wearing matching bottoms."

Baldy grunts in agreement as his dark eyes watch his partner undo the button and zipper of my jeans.

"Get your filthy hands off me!" I scream in frustration.

I pull at every bit of strength in me, but it isn't enough to throw a fully grown man off myself.

T opens the front of my jeans and smiles wickedly. "You dirty girl." His tone deepens with want as he takes in the matching dark purple lace underwear.

He hooks his calloused fingers in the pocket of my jeans and begins to tug them down my hips.

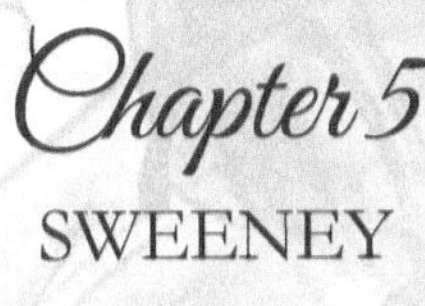

Chapter 5
SWEENEY

The sound of a woman's blood-curdling scream yanks me from sleep. My eyes fly open, and my hands grip the black throwing knives I leave hidden beneath my pillow. I've always preferred knives over guns, choosing to fight up close and personal rather than from afar. That's how I got my call sign.

Each one of us on the team at Hunter's company, Red Sky Security, is given one. They are unique in their own way. Whether it be a physical attribute, personality trait, or something that happened that was so memorable, good or bad, that the nickname stuck.

Hunter is known as Boss. The reason is self-explanatory. Einstein, because he's a tech wiz, hacker, and certified genius. He's our eyes and ears behind the scenes while we're away guarding clients. Fuse is an explosives expert. Anything that goes boom, he's our man. Doc, named after the infamous gunslinger Doc Holliday, is a sharpshooter. If you need a sniper watching your back, he's your guy. And myself, named after the fictional serial killer from the mid-1800s, Sweeney Todd. He was a barber who killed people with straight razors.

I slip my index fingers through the circular hole on the end of the hilt, twirl them around, and grip them firmly as I leap from my bed in nothing but my boxers.

I throw open my bedroom door and enter the darkened hallway, only nightlights placed sporadically down the hall illuminate small amounts of the carpet. I know my home like the back of my hand, so I don't bother flipping on lights as I clear the upper level, swiftly moving from room to room.

I'm just passing the spare bathroom when I hear the scream again. The blood drains from my face. I'd recognize it anywhere. It's Addi. That time I heard it in Hawaii in those woods as she tried to fight off those two criminals is etched into my long-term memory. I couldn't forget it, even if I tried.

I push open her door and enter the room, knives at the ready to fling at anything I see moving or trying to lurk in the shadows. My gaze sweeps across the space, but no one's there. Then my vision zeroes in on the dark form lying in the middle of the bed.

Addi lies there, covers askew from thrashing in her sleep. A nightmare. That's all it is. I know them all too well. I release a breath, gently place the knives down atop her nightstand, and sit on the edge of her bed.

"No, please…" she mumbles and whimpers, gently turning her head from side to side, eyelids clenched tightly. "Please… No! No!" Her screams grow louder, and her thrashing becomes more frantic.

Sweat has beaded up along her brows, and her brown and blonde hair is mussed. The sight before me leaves me feeling as if my heart was ripped out and stomped on. I hate that she has to suffer through this. I wish I could've been the one to kill Jack. I wish that fucker never existed on this earth, but at least he's gone for good, hopefully burning somewhere in hell.

I hope he's being tortured down there, day and night, forced to relive his worst fears in an endless loop while demons carve up his flesh before they heal him and start again. Over and over. That thought alone brings me much pleasure. It's the least he deserves after everything he did to Addi and Serenity.

I gently grip her shoulders and focus on keeping my voice steady and calm. "Addi, wake up." Her pleas and thrashing continue, so I try again. "Addi, you're having a nightmare. Wake up." Again, her murmurs continue. "Addison, listen to the sound of my voice. What you are experiencing is a dream, sweetheart. You're safe. I promise I won't let anything happen to you. Wake up, sweetheart. Open those beautiful eyes for me."

At that, her chocolate eyes shoot open, and she gasps for air as if she were drowning and finally broke the surface. I keep my hold against her shoulders, gentle but firm, trying to get her to see she's safe and unharmed.

"Eyes on me, Addison. Slow, deep breaths," I coach her through her panic, never once letting my gentle voice falter.

After half a minute, her breathing seems to even out, and her eyes become more focused as they glue to mine.

"I'm sorry I woke you." Her voice is hoarse from screaming.

I release my grip on her shoulders and place my hands on each side of her legs as she sits up and leans against the headboard, pulling the covers up around her waist. I release a long breath and run my fingers through my hair.

"You have nothing to be sorry for. Everyone has nightmares now and again." She stays quiet as she drops her gaze and begins to pick at the edge of the comforter. "How often do they happen?"

I brace myself because I know I won't like the answer she voices. Call it a gut feeling. Or maybe it's experience.

"Every time I sleep…" Her voice is so quiet, and the look in her eyes makes it feel like someone is squeezing my heart in their fist.

"Is it always the same one? Or different ones?"

"It's always the same two. Sometimes it will be me and Renny standing in the middle of that living room while Jack confesses his ugly truth. His hurtful words are playing on repeat and spearing through my heart over and over."

Her voice cracks at the end, and she takes a breath, fighting to remain in control of her emotions. Tears line her chocolate eyes, but they don't fall. I place a hand on her right shin bone, only allowing this contact, over the covers, to let her know that I'm here. That she's here in this room with me. Safe. My thumb strokes back and forth over the bone while I wait patiently for her to continue.

After a minute, she does. "As horrible as it sounds, I prefer the first one, but the other times it's me jumping out of that trunk and running through the woods with those two thugs chasing me. They always catch me and hurt me. Sometimes I wake up there. Other times… In my nightmares, what you did, how you saved me, it doesn't happen. If I don't wake myself up, it continues from the point of them ripping off my clothes and…"

"Shh…" I gently cup her chin and swipe my thumb over the tear that escaped her hold. "You don't have to finish. I understand." Her glossy eyes meet mine, and she sucks her bottom lip between her teeth, causing the fist around my heart to tighten its hold. "None of that happened. Alright? That's your mind playing tricks on you. I *was* there that day. I *did* stop them. You got out and are safe now. So, when your mind starts pushing the dream further, take control and force it to stop. Remember what truly happened and let it stop there."

Addi nods her head and another lonely tear escapes. I swipe it away like I did the last one.

"Thank you." Her lips quiver, and she throws her arms around me.

My body tenses at first, not wanting to scare her with a simple touch or contact of any kind. But as her grip tightens around my neck, I relax and wrap a strong arm around her middle, pulling her closer to me. She loses the battle with her tears as she sobs into my shoulder.

I don't try to say anything else. Unfortunately, there are no words that would instantly heal her trauma. No matter how badly I wish that were possible. I simply allow my presence to soothe her in the way she needs it most. Allowing it to be confirmation that she's safe. I hold her and stroke her hair with my free hand, never letting up on my secure grip around her waist. After a while, I feel her begin to settle down and relax. Only when I feel her start to pull back do I release my arm from around her.

"You should try to get some rest." I move to stand, but her hand around my forearm halts me.

I peer down at her touch, loving the feel of her skin against mine before glancing up and meeting her gaze.

"Will you stay with me? Just until I fall back asleep. *If* I'm able to fall back asleep."

She bites her lip nervously, and it takes everything in me not to suck it into my mouth and bite it myself.

"Are you sure? I don't want to… make you uncomfortable." My tone is hesitant.

I should say no. Every bone inside my body is screaming at me to do so. I know that's the right thing to do, but I honestly don't think I can ever tell this woman no. If she asked me to have sex with her right now, I'd be apprehensive, but eventually, I'd cave. I'd give this woman the world on a silver platter if she asked me to.

A bubble of shaky laughter rolls up her throat, causing my brows to rise.

"You're the last person that would ever make me uncomfortable, Grayson."

And there it is. Right fucking there. The piece of straw that's broken my will. My name on her lips will forever be my undoing. Maybe I shouldn't have told her my real name. Ah, hell. There's no going back now. I'm a glutton for punishment indeed. I don't trust my voice, so I give her a nod, stand, and cross to the other side of the bed.

"On top or under the covers?" I question.

"Which would you prefer? I'd figure you'd get cold if you slept on top of them." Her gaze slowly drops down my mostly naked frame, and when she reaches my boxers, they snap back up to mine.

I give her a sly grin. "This is your show, sweetheart. You make the rules."

"We're adults. Well, I am, at least. I'm still on the fence about you." She pulls a laugh from me, loving that some of her smartass has returned. "I think we can both sleep beneath the covers and remain mature about it."

"Speak for yourself." I shoot her a wink. "I'm a snuggler. So, you've been warned."

I shrug my shoulder and slide beneath the covers, making sure not to let our bare legs touch as we both settle in, lying on our sides and facing each other.

"Good night, Grayson."

She gives me a smile that seems just a fraction lighter than this morning. I'll take that as progress.

"Good night, sweetheart."

I watch as her warm vision slowly drifts closed, and if I'm being honest with myself, I can't tear my gaze away. I revel in the way her rounded features slacken as she relaxes into sleep like she has no care in the world. As if she weren't betrayed by a man who vowed to love her until death do they part, then be forced to fend off attempted murder by not just one, but two fully grown men. The only reason I stop watching the sleeping beauty next to me is because my eyes grow heavy, and I finally drift off to sleep.

The delectable smell of ripe strawberries rouses me. I snuggle further into the warmth that surrounds me, chasing that sweet berry scent. As my eyes crack open, I find myself snuggled into the back of a goddess, my face buried in her highlighted strands. I lift my face enough to see my arm draped around her middle and our bodies flush against each other. Her back to my chest.

I bring my nose closer to her hair and take a deep breath. *Fucking strawberries.* God, if I could only smell one thing for the rest of my life, it would be this. By her steady, shallow breathing, Addi's still asleep. She hadn't woken up again from another nightmare and... neither did I.

Not that my nightmares have me screaming or thrashing in my sleep. At least, not for the last several years. Once I graduated high school, I thought about joining the military, but I happened to come across an ad for Academi. A company that provides contract security services for the US federal government. It sounded like a better option, so I applied and worked for them for nearly seven years before meeting Boss.

After he learned of my... abilities, he offered me a job at a company he'd just started. Red Sky Security. What truly intrigued me was the chance to travel but still maintain a permanent settlement here in Oklahoma so that I can be with my family again after so many years away with Academi.

At first, my nightmares used to wake me almost every night and I'd be drenched in sweat. Over the years and with some professional help, I've learned to master them. I still get them, don't get me wrong, but I've learned to take control and wake myself up. Now they're just a nuisance.

I didn't have one while sleeping in here with Addi. In fact, my dream was rather... pleasant. Which I haven't experienced since I was a teenager, before tainting my soul with the profession I chose upon entering adulthood.

I allow myself one more breath of her intoxicating aroma and begin to slowly remove myself from the bed. I don't want to wake her. She needs all the rest she can get. Who knows just how much sleep she's gotten this last week if she has a nightmare every time she closes her eyes? Three square meals a day and eight hours of sleep each night. Challenge accepted.

With this new goal stamped into my mind with determination, I stand from the bed and quickly adjust my erection to a more concealed position in case she wakes up and finds me still in nothing but my boxers. Trying to explain my morning wood might be a little awkward. Well, awkward for her, not for me. I'm proud of what I've been blessed with, and I've never had any complaints.

I'm almost to the door when I remember my knives. How could I forget my babies? I gently pick them up, murmur my apologies to them, and make my way out of the room, easing the door closed behind me. I let out a breath of relief as I walk back down the hallway to my room so I can brush my teeth and dress for the day. When I'm ready, I head downstairs to start breakfast.

Chapter 6
ADDISON

My eyes slowly flutter awake as I yawn and send myself into a big stretch. I turn to my other side and glance toward the window. Hints of sunlight try to break through the shut blinds. It takes me a minute to realize that I feel… good. After a week of little to no sleep, I feel rested. Well, not fully, but more so than I have this last week. So, I'll count it as a win.

After taking a deep breath, I drop my gaze to the empty space beside me. My hand drifts over the mattress, finding it still warm, as if Grayson left only minutes ago. A small smile tugs at the corner of my mouth at the thought of him keeping his movements quiet so he wouldn't wake me.

My ex never did that. He always woke before me, having to be at the firm before my job at the bank started. He'd flick on lights if he were searching for something, open doors without a care, and sometimes have videos or music playing on his phone while he got ready. He was never rude with it. He'd keep the volume low, but he could've taken more care. I'd spoken to him about it on several occasions, but he'd always shrug innocently as if he didn't see what he was doing as wrong. As if his morning routine was stamped in stone and couldn't be changed.

Once the sleep fog is fully gone from my mind, I realize that I didn't have another nightmare. This is the first time in a week, since everything happened on that island, that I slept and didn't wake up screaming or covered in sweat, clutching at my chest and gasping for breath as if it were being stolen from me. I don't know what changed things.

Maybe it's being in a new place. Maybe it was talking and opening up to Grayson. Or maybe… Maybe it was because Grayson slept next to me. Though my relationship trust has been ruined, my non-relationship trust is still somewhat intact. And since Grayson has already proven with his actions—that speak louder than words ever could—that he's willing to protect me, maybe somewhere deep in my psyche, that helped me to relax enough to not live in a constant state of fear?

I mull over that thought as I leave my room and enter the bathroom. I wash the sleep from my face with cold water that has me gasping from the shock before I brush my teeth and brush out my hair. After throwing it up into a messy bun, I open the door and head downstairs.

The smell of food cooking hits me halfway down, and my mouth waters with anticipation. I didn't lie last night when I told Grayson that I hadn't had much of an appetite since everything that happened. However, being here, with him, in this new and safe environment has me slowly looking forward to each meal. Maybe it's his cooking? Which is surprisingly amazing. I'd never tell him that though. If his ego got any larger, he'd need a bigger house.

I hit the hardwood floors, round the corner, and pad down the hallway. He has the news playing on the mounted flatscreen with the volume turned low. They're discussing the seven-day forecast, and by the looks of it, we're in for some storms and hot, muggy weather. Great. Gotta love Oklahoma summers.

The scent of breakfast grows stronger as I enter the kitchen and take a seat at the same barstool I did last night. If Grayson knows I'm here, he doesn't let on. His back is to me as he flips what looks like French toast over on the griddle part of the stove top, which is bordered by two gas burners on each side.

Thankfully, he put on some clothes. He's in the pajamas he wore last night. Black pajama bottoms and a dark green T-shirt. A part of me is sad to see that body of his covered up, but the other part is thankful. When I woke last night and saw him in nothing but his boxers, I thought I had died and gone to hell. Hell, because there's no way heaven has angels that look as sinful as him.

Jack was tall with lean muscles and was handsome enough to model, but this man… Grayson's body puts Jack's to shame. I don't understand how it's physically possible to have so many muscles in one body, each one well-defined and honed with years of labor and hard work. He's taller and broader, with colorful ink snaking up his right arm that makes you want to trace every line with your tongue.

And when my eyes drifted to his waistline, his boxers left little to the imagination of what lay beneath the thin fabric. He wasn't hard. That would have been inappropriate, given the circumstances of last night. But the normal size of it left my brain trying to imagine its full power and might. I had to quickly look away and scold myself for even peeking. I'm in no position to start something with anyone. I need to work on myself first. I feel I'm going to need to repeat that little mantra to myself for the next few weeks until my hormones fall into line.

"Would you like some coffee?" he calls over his shoulder without glancing at me.

Well, that answers my earlier question about whether he knew I was sitting here or not.

"I can get it." I go to stand, but his next word stops me.

"Sit."

I don't know why my body instinctively listens, but I do just that. He plates the toast before finally turning and moving toward the coffee maker. He reaches into an upper cabinet and pulls down one of my favorite coffee mugs. My mouth parts in shock. I put them in there last night after he went to bed, when I was unpacking my things. How'd he know they were there?

"How do you like it?"

"Depends on my mood." I release a weak, playful sigh. "Some days I want strong and dominating, others I want slow and gentle."

He arches a brow at me, and a grin pulls at one side of his full lips. "Your coffee, sweetheart."

"Oh." I feign disappointment but can't stop the small twitch of my lips. "A scoop of sugar and a splash of milk, please."

"I'm not familiar with that measurement." He chuckles as he pours the coffee and adds sugar. "Please explain how much a 'splash' is."

"You know, you pour the milk, count to two really quick, and stop." He shakes his head, retrieves the milk, and does just that. "It's an official measuring technique. Didn't you learn about it in school?"

"I must've been absent that day." He chuckles and places the steaming cup in front of me. "Nice mug, by the way."

He nods to the white ceramic cup with a black handle and words that read, *Of course your feelings matter. Just not to me.* I clutch it in my palms, blow lightly over it, and take a small sip. I love snarky coffee mugs. Anytime Serenity finds one she knows I'll love, she'll gift it to me.

"How did you know it was there? I put it away after you went to bed last night."

"Nothing goes unnoticed in my house."

I hum quietly to myself. "Does that mean you know about the toy I have in my dresser drawer?"

He nearly drops the plate but recovers quickly. I can't help but laugh to myself. I love messing with him. It's the highlight of my days. At least I know living with him is going to be fun.

I don't miss the way his eyes darken as he peers at me, but his face is schooled as he says, "I hope you like French toast." His words are strained as he holds up a plate with two thick slices stacked on it. I smile and nod as he questions, "Powder sugar? Syrup?"

"Yes, and syrup on the side, please. I'm a dunker, not a soaker."

"Noted." He hands me the plate and a small sauce bowl filled with warm syrup. "Do you have a game plan?"

I cut a slice of French toast and dip it in the syrup before plopping it in my mouth. My eyes close and a small moan of satisfaction vibrates in my throat as I relish the explosion of flavors. This man can easily make me fat with his cooking. I open my eyes to find him chewing his own breakfast, but his vision is narrowed in on my mouth. My tongue darts out to lick them clean, and his eyes follow the movement. His jaw ticks once, twice, before his eyes shift to mine.

It takes me a minute to remember he asked me a question. "Game plan for what, exactly?"

"Torturing your enemies, world domination. You know, those sorts of ambitions," he teases.

But I know what he means. What's my game plan with life? Where do I go from here? What's my first step?

"Honestly, I have no clue." I sigh heavily and take another bite. "I'll have to return to work, but I still have another week. I scheduled two weeks off for the wedding, so…" I trail off, not wanting to continue that line of thought.

The food in my mouth turns acidic as I swallow and wash it down with some coffee.

"Good." He nods approvingly. "That gives you plenty of time before you have to reemerge back in public."

"Maybe I should reach out? Look into getting some professional help?"

"If you feel it would help, do it."

"Have you ever… sought help?" I inquire cautiously.

"Yes." He doesn't hesitate. "It's how I learned to master my own demons."

I nod but remain quiet as I take another bite. A part of me wishes so desperately to dive deeper into that. I can only picture the sort of demons he has wreaking havoc within him. But surprisingly, I'm not scared. I'm merely curious. Wanting to know the deepest darkest truths of my new roommate's soul.

"When do you have to go back to work?" I inquire around another bite.

"Tomorrow."

Again, I remain quiet and nod. Will it be weird being here alone all day? Will I feel awkward being left to my own devices in someone else's home? I only pray the quiet doesn't grow too loud. And that Sharleen stays hidden. *Please let him have been joking about her.* I stifle a chill as my eyes discreetly scan the kitchen and living room, thankful that I don't find an old lady apparition floating nearby.

"How would you like to spend the day? Shall we draw up a plan for world domination, or would you like to be lazy and binge some TV?" He hikes a brow in challenge, and his whisky eyes sparkle with mischief.

"Oh, I've already got detailed plans. I even laminated them to keep them safe." I give him a small smile. "But spending the day watching TV does sound therapeutic."

"Your will shall be done, my lady." Grayson gives me a mocking bow before taking my empty plate and his and placing them in the sink.

We do, in fact, spend the entire day on his sofa. I don't know how, maybe he's got a hidden superpower, but he was able to coax out my confession about my love for reality dating shows. As well as my fear of ever watching them again. However, he insisted that I couldn't keep letting Jack take things or ruin things that used to bring me joy.

We binged an entire season of *Dating Naked*, ordered greasy pizza, and didn't move from that couch unless it was for bathroom breaks or to get fresh beers. I feared I wouldn't enjoy myself, knowing I watched these things with Jack, but thinking back on it, I didn't think about that piece of shit once. Anytime I'm around Grayson, Jack is the furthest from my mind. I can't even begin to understand why it is, but I'm not about to start questioning it.

Long after the sun sets, Grayson peers at the time on his phone and winces. "It's getting late, and I have to be up early. We should call it a night."

I agree and help him clean up by placing any leftover pizza in the fridge and tossing our empty beer bottles in the trash. I've been toying with an idea in my head. A theory, really, that has my nerves kicking into overdrive as I ascend the stairs with Grayson following behind me.

As we reach the landing, I turn to face him and take a deep breath. He notices the shift in me, and his gaze drops to where I pick at the hem of my shirt. The shirt he lent me yesterday that I can't get myself to return to him just yet. It smells like him, like cedar and fresh rain, and for some unknown reason, I find it soothing.

"What's up? Having second thoughts about world domination?"

"No." I snort and take another breath. "After I woke from my nightmare and you agreed to stay, I didn't have another one. For the first time since everything happened, I truly slept. So…"

His eyes are locked on mine, his features kept in his casual, charismatic attitude as he waits patiently for me to continue.

"I have a theory that…" *Ugh, why is this so hard to ask? Why can't I find the right words?* A sigh of frustration slips out, causing my shoulders to drop. I go for a straight and honest approach. No beating around the bush. "Can you sleep with me again? Just for tonight? I want to see if it was a fluke blessing or if… If your presence helped me."

He remains quiet as his honey gaze roams over my rounded features as if weighing every pro and con of my experiment. The seconds drag on like minutes, and my nerves have my stomach twisting into a tight knot.

"Never mind, just forget about it. It was a silly idea. Good night."

The words spill out of my mouth after my nerves win the battle and I chicken out. Not able to bear a possible rejection. I quickly spin on my heel, take long, quick strides to the bathroom, and shut the door, letting out a defeated sigh as my back rests against the wood.

I close my eyes and curse myself for crossing a line, for pushing a boundary that needs to stay firmly in place between us. It's fine. I'll learn to fight my demons on my own. I'm a big girl. People do this alone every day. Why should I be any different?

I quickly run through my nightly routine before exiting the bathroom, nearly running into a brick wall. Grayson is leaning against the frame with his arms crossed over his chest and an eyebrow arched high.

"Shit!" I gasp and clutch my chest, feeling my heart pounding erratically beneath. "You scared the crap out of me."

"Well, you ran like a coward before I could answer."

"I… Um…"

I haven't the slightest clue what to say. He's not afraid to call out my bullshit. Noted. So, I straighten my spine and tilt my chin up to meet his gaze. Though I'm tall for a woman, standing at five-foot-eight, he's got a good half a foot on me, at least.

I clear my throat and will steadiness into my voice. "What's your answer then?"

"I'm willing to test your theory. Count me intrigued."

"Okay then." I give him a curt nod and brush past him, entering my bedroom.

I don't need to turn around to know he's following close behind. I can feel his presence like the security blanket I'm becoming too used to. I plug my phone into the charger and turn to see him standing with his feet shoulder-width apart, arms crossed over his chest, and his head cocked to the side as if lost in thought.

My voice is hesitant as I question, "Is something wrong?"

"No." He doesn't tear his vision away from the dresser as he answers. "Just trying to figure out which drawer your toy is in." My phone fumbles out of my hand and lands atop the nightstand with a loud *thud,* but still, he doesn't break his concentration. "Are you the kind to store it in the top drawer for easy access and uncaring if someone sees it? Or are you the kind to hide it in the bottom drawer, far in the back and buried under piles of clothes as if you're ashamed you even own it."

"Shouldn't you already know? Nothing goes unnoticed in your house, remember?" I quote his earlier words from breakfast.

I watch his shoulders shake with laughter as he finally moves to the other side of the bed and begins stripping down to his boxers.

"What are you doing?"

My tone rises an octave with nerves, and my words are shaky as I try to look away but find myself unable to. If he's willing to strip in front of me, I have a right to watch. Period.

"Going to bed. I can't sleep in clothes. They're too constricting." He doesn't even look at me as he drops his clothes in a pile next to the bed, leaving only his boxers on.

Holy fuck… This man puts Greek gods' bodies to shame.

"You didn't seem to care last night."

I clear my throat. "Alright. Then I can do the same?"

His gaze snaps up, and his hands halt halfway from throwing back the covers. His vision slowly trails down my front and back up. "Feel free to sleep in any manner of clothing. Or lack of."

I catch the way his voice drops an octave, and my knees nearly wobble, sending a foreign flutter through my stomach.

"You're such a perv." I huff out a laugh and shake my head clear.

We both slide beneath the covers and fall into a comfortable silence. Before I know it, my eyelids flutter closed, and sleep overtakes me.

Chapter 7
ADDISON

"Jack? What's going on?" I ask in disbelief as my body visibly begins to tremble.

Jack stands there with his legs spread apart and his hands tucked casually into the pockets of his slacks. "Isn't it obvious?"

"No… it can't be," Serenity mumbles. "You're my… intruder?" she asks hesitantly, her voice barely above a whisper.

Both kidnappers file into the living room, remove the bindings from our wrists, and take a seat on the couch. They lean back and watch the scene unfold in front of them as if they're watching a movie and not two people's lives being torn apart at the seams.

I whip my head toward my friend, my eyes wide at the accusation. "Of course not! Honey, tell her she's wrong." When Jack doesn't say anything, I snap my head back toward my husband, any faster and I'd risk a broken neck. "J-Jack? Renny's wrong… right?"

"She's not wrong." Jack shrugs his shoulders, acting as if he hadn't just ripped out and stomped all over my heart.

I remain silent, my jaw slightly parted, and a numbness settles over my body. An intense war between my heart and head begins to wage within.

"Why?" Serenity shouts at him, demanding answers. "How could you do this to her?"

Jack's emerald gaze holds Serenity's bottle-green eyes prisoner. "Because it's you, Renny. It's been you from the start. She was just a means to an end."

Serenity closes the space between herself and Jack and slaps him, the sound echoing in the otherwise silent space. It pulls me back to reality, and I gasp in shock.

T goes to stand up, but Jack holds out his hand, stopping him. "It's alright. Emotions are high right now."

He gently rubs his clean-shaven cheek, smoothing out the sting from the slap.

"How could you say that about your wife? My best friend!" Serenity balls her fists at her side.

"It is what it is," Jack states calmly. "I won't sugarcoat anything, and I won't lie."

"But… I love you, and… I know you love me," I say in a quiet voice that's filled with disbelief. If the room hadn't been dead silent, no one would have heard it.

"Jesus, you must have those rose-colored glasses glued on, don't you? I never loved you." Jack has the audacity to laugh. Serenity swings, but he catches it this time. "I allowed the first one, but you will not hit me again."

Serenity yanks her arm out of his grasp and takes a few steps back, coming to a stop beside me.

"That's a fucking lie!" I shout in denial. "You wouldn't have married me if you didn't love me."

We share over two years of history together. There's no way he could have been faking our entire relationship. His actions over the years proved he loved me… Right? The fact that I could've been entirely wrong about him makes me want to vomit, but I clamp my jaw tight, resisting to submit.

"I was only with you to get close to Renny," he confesses, keeping his calm demeanor.

"Explain yourself. Now!" Serenity grits out through clenched teeth.

"When I first saw you, your beauty lured me into a trap like a siren's sweet melody. I knew immediately that you were the one I wanted. Unfortunately, I realized you were otherwise… unavailable at the moment because of Noah." He locks eyes with Serenity again. "When I learned the two of you were as close as sisters, I saw an opportunity that Addi could provide for me, so I took it. By pretending to date her, I got to be around you all the time. Each time we hung out, I fell further for you. Your beauty, your intelligence, your wit, your kind heart. I loved it all. I thought Noah was a fling, but when I realized how serious the two of y'all were becoming, I knew I had to get him out of the picture."

"What do you mean you had to get him out of the picture?" Serenity asks wearily.

Jack's grin turns ominous. "I paid a prostitute to sleep with him. Knowing how big trust is to you, I knew you would dump him, and boy was I ecstatic when you did."

"But we were already engaged at that time. How do you explain that?" I throw in.

"We had reached the point in our 'relationship,'" he uses air quotes for the word as if none of it was real, "where it was time for me to propose if I wanted to keep you around. If I lost you, I lost her." He motions his head toward Serenity.

"Then why go through with marrying her? Why not find a reason to postpone it so you didn't get locked in?" Serenity interrogates him further.

His eyes darken as a wicked expression crosses his pointed features. "Because it would look less suspicious to the cops."

"Wh—what?" I stagger back as if his words physically struck me.

"I took out a multi-million dollar life insurance policy on you, my dear wife. I married you so I would look less suspicious to the cops when I hired people to kill you the day after our wedding. You would be surprised at the number of criminals I've defended who had killed their partners for the money. I learned from their mistakes and formulated an airtight plan that would not tie anything back to me."

No… It can't be true. It just can't be! I keep trying to pinch myself, hoping that this is all just some horrible nightmare, but it's not. Jack, the man I've devoted years of my life to, the man I vowed to love until death do us part, had orchestrated a ploy to kill me… for money… so he could be with who he truly loved. Renny. My palms begin to sweat, my pulse skyrockets, and my stomach churns.

"You sick fuck!" Serenity shouts. "Why would you ever do that?"

"For us!" Jack's voice rises with desperation, piercing Serenity with his heated gaze. "I quit my job at the firm and bought this house. Our house, Renny. After the authorities discover my poor wife's body, I'll collect the money so we can live here comfortably, just the two of us. I wanted enough time alone with you to help you adjust and to make up for all the lost years we should have been together."

He takes a step toward Serenity, but her cringe has him pausing.

"What makes you think I would ever be with you? Especially after I knew what you did to my best friend."

"You don't have a choice, Renny. Given enough time, you'll warm up to me. I'll prove that I'm nothing like those cheating men you keep getting involved with," he throws at her, knowing the fresh memory of Hunter's betrayal still stings.

"But you paid another woman to kiss Hunter last night. He didn't do anything wrong!" I defend Hunter.

I'll be damned if I let him sully the name of a truly good man. A man I pray is looking for us right now. A man that Jack could take a few pointers from about being a decent fucking human being. But after all this, I fear Jack is beyond saving.

Serenity gasps. "What?"

"It was to prove that if the temptation presented itself to them, any man would give in to it. I would never do that to you, Renny. I've been loyal to you from the start, and I always will be." He speaks to Serenity with full confidence in his voice.

"Loyal to me?" Serenity scoffs. "Jack, you were living and sleeping with my best friend, just to get to me. How is that loyalty?"

"Because every time I was with her, I pictured it was you!" Jack's voice rises another octave. As if noticing it, he takes a deep breath and releases it slowly.

The confession hits us like a bird flying into a windshield. Hard and ugly.

"What the fuck!" I shout, now that I've had some time for the shock to wear off. I'm beyond pissed.

Jack turns to me and speaks calmly. "Didn't you ever wonder why I never said your name during sex or usually buried my face in the crook of your neck?"

"I thought it was weird at first, but I just figured it was one of your quirks."

"It's because if I said a name while coming, it would have been Renny's name on my lips, not yours, and there was no getting around trying to explain that one. Anytime I entered you, fucked you, came inside of you, I pictured it was her I was doing all those things to. You were just a hole to use."

"You fucking bastard!" I storm toward him and slap him. He allows the first one but catches my wrist when I go to swing a second time. "Did a part of you ever love me?" My voice breaks as tears fall in rivers down my cheeks, and realization hits me about the sickening truth of the man I'd chosen as my life partner. "Was there any part of this that was real?"

"No," he says to me coldly. "I think we're done here. Gentleman," Jack calls to the two men still sitting on the couch, "she's all yours. You know what to do."

"Addi!" Serenity yells as Baldy bends down and throws me over his shoulder as if I were nothing but a measly sack of potatoes to him.

"Don't fucking touch me! Let me go!" I scream as I flail around in his grasp. I use every ounce of strength inside of me to kick my legs and pound my fists into his meaty back. I might as well have been a child for how little my struggle affects him. "Renny!" I scream as he hauls me to their car with his partner shutting the door behind us as we leave.

"You can kick and scream all you want, girly, but your fate has been sealed," T says as he places a quick smack to my ass as he passes by, and pops open the trunk of their car.

My eyes widen as panic and fear hit me. I would be taking the ride in that darkened, cramped space. "Don't you dare put me in there!"

Before I'm thrown into the trunk, the world around me begins to blur and fade away. I feel myself being set down on my feet as I shield my eyes from a blinding light. Suddenly, my shoes are gone, and I feel soft, warm sand between my toes. I peer up to find myself standing on a beach, with only the sound of the waves crashing against the shore to fill my ears.

My clothes have changed. Gone were the jeans and tank top I wore the day of my almost murder. They're replaced by a loose white tank top and a pair of black shorts that stop mid-thigh. The gentle sea breeze blows my loose strands elegantly around my shoulders.

I feel the rage from Jack's confession, and the fear of being taken into those woods by T and Baldy leave my body. A sense of peace settles over me, relaxing my heart, mind, and soul. I feel a presence approach me, and like always, I know who it is without looking.

Grayson comes to a stop beside me, his gaze trained on the horizon. I turn my head and take in his appearance. This is the most casual I've ever seen him, barefoot, dressed in a dark grey T-shirt and a pair of tan cargo shorts. I peer up at him, loving the way the sun highlights his golden skin and sharp features. Finally, he turns his head to glance at me, his eyes sparkling like the most expensive yellow topaz. A genuine smile lifts his lips back and my heart hitches.

I feel his large hand slip into mine as he interlocks our fingers and squeezes my hand. The touch is gentle but firm, as if silently communicating that I'm safe and free. I tear my eyes away and peer out toward the horizon, loving the simple feeling of him standing next to me, loving the calmness his presence allows me to feel. And for a long while, we stand there in silence, gazing out at the crystal blue waters.

Chapter 8
SWEENEY

When Addi asked me to partake in her little experiment, I knew without a doubt I'd say yes. Although an internal war was waging—my brain screaming no, my heart screaming yes—I knew which would win in the end. But the woman took my hesitation as a no and ran. All I could do was shake my head and chuckle as I watched her disappear into the bathroom.

Lying next to her in bed was like a feeling I'd never experienced before. After living twenty-seven years on this earth, I thought I'd experienced peace before, but having Addi at my side proved how incredibly wrong I was. It felt like every decision I made in life had led me here. It felt like this woman was my female counterpart, like we're two peas in a pod, like our souls, when combined, made a perfect whole. It felt... right.

And damn, if that didn't scare the shit out of me. I've done a lot of dating in my day, had a few girlfriends, and slept around more than I should have, but never did I feel as if any of those women could be anything more than a good time. Anything permanent. But when I saw Addi enter that bar, I just knew. I know how fucking cheesy that must sound, but I'm now a firm believer in love at first sight.

The little blue sundress she wore clung to her curves and showed off a teasing amount of her thick thighs. Skinny girls are fine, but I prefer my women with a little meat on their bones. Addi's got that athletic build, and damn if the sight of her full ass and plump exposed cleavage didn't go straight to my groin.

I wasn't lying when I introduced myself to her and said she was the most beautiful woman I'd ever met. In my line of work, I've felt pain and loss before. But when Boss told me she was getting married the next week, the devastation was almost unbearable. I didn't cross any lines, but the longer I talked to her, the further I fell.

The last thing I remembered was watching her sleep, resisting the urge to tuck a few stray strands behind her ear, before I was roused by her tossing and turning. Thankfully, it wasn't as violent as last night, so I did the only thing I could think of. I rolled to my side and pulled her back flush against my chest.

She didn't fight me, and she didn't wake. After I draped an arm around her waist and buried my face in her hair, breathing in her intoxicating strawberry scent, I felt her begin to settle as she nestled further into my warmth. I didn't bother stopping the smile of satisfaction that tugged at my lips at knowing that simply holding her was enough to calm her.

A sleepy sigh escaped her lips that tugged at my heartstrings. I knew I was no more than putty in her hands. A few minutes later, I drifted back to sleep and didn't move or wake until my alarm sounded the next morning.

I reach over and shut it off before peering back at the goddess in my arms, still sound asleep. I allow myself one more deep inhale of her scent before carefully rising from the bed and leaving to get ready for work.

If we have a meeting with clients, we dress professionally in a dress shirt and a pair of slacks. But we have none today, so I throw on workout clothes. A pair of black shorts and a dark red stringer tank top. After drinking some coffee, I place my cup in the sink, put my shoes on, and enter the garage.

I press the glowing red button on the wall and bright morning rays begin to illuminate the dark room. As I slide on my black motorcycle helmet and fasten the strap beneath my chin, I can't help but grin as I observe the beautiful, bright blue, newer model Dodge Challenger with black accents that now resides in my driveway.

I'm not surprised by Addi's taste in cars. Somehow, I couldn't picture her driving anything else. I put my red and black Honda CBR in neutral and walk it out of the garage before roaring it to life, trying my best not to wake the woman still asleep upstairs.

I lose myself on my ride to work, loving the wind rushing past as I weave through the morning traffic. It's one of the pros of riding a bike that I'm particularly fond of. Before I know it, I'm pulling into the parking lot of Red Sky Security. It's a large, standalone brick building with bulletproof windows lining the front.

"Good morning, Sweeney," Phoebe, a young woman with rounded features, light blonde hair with baby blue highlights, and colorful glasses, greets me from behind a dark mahogany receptionist's desk.

"Good morning, Blue." I shoot her a playful wink.

When Boss started the company, he had hired a woman who'd put more effort into trying to sleep with all of us rather than focusing on her job. We never gave her the time of day for many reasons, but most importantly, we respected his no-workplace dating rule. He had talked to her multiple times, telling her to stop, and had given her far too many chances before inevitably firing her.

Boss then hired Phoebe, and she's been with us ever since. In nearly two years, she hasn't once looked at any of us with the slightest bit of want in her grey eyes. Well, except for Einstein. I may not be as observant as Boss, but I've noticed the longing glances she gives Einstein when she believes no one is looking. It's not one-sided either. Einstein has had a thing for her from day one, but also respects Boss's rule.

The lobby is bright and open, with a neutral grey coloring the walls and black armchairs lining the back wall. Dark hardwood floors lie horizontally, helping the space to appear bigger. To my right is a hallway of offices lining both sides, one for each of us. Boss's is the biggest and is located at the end of the hall.

After placing my helmet atop my desk in my office, I walk through large wooden double doors that lead to a spacious briefing room with a massive dark wood conference table. I keep going back through another door that leads to our fully stocked armory and Einstein's office, which resides off to the side. Boss has offered him a space by ours numerous times, but the evil genius likes his privacy.

I find Boss and the little genius in the private gym off the back.

"Hey," both Boss and Einstein greet me in unison.

Einstein curls up in a crunch atop a mat on the floor, hands interlocked behind his head, before he blows out a breath and flattens out to ready for another. Boss straddles a bench, doing preacher curls. His biceps bulge against his skin, and prominent veins snake down both arms, heavily painted with dark ink.

"Evil genius." I nod toward Einstein, who shows me his middle finger but grins. "Big Daddy." I wiggle my brows at Boss, who rolls his eyes and shakes his head, not stopping until he finishes his set.

Fuse and Doc are out on jobs, so it's just the three of us. If we aren't out on assignments, our normal work week consists of a morning workout, followed by sparring and rolling on mats set up in the back. We do this to help stay in shape and to help keep our fighting techniques sharp. Then, we're free to go home.

Honestly, Boss is the best person I've ever worked for. For more reasons than one. After a killer leg workout and some cardio, the three of us take turns sparring and rolling with each other. Though Einstein doesn't ever leave the office for assignments and never fights, he still works out with us to stay in shape.

For some ungodly reason, the little fucker's ground game is a force to be reckoned with. Though he has muscles, it must be his lean frame that helps him slip out of holds, and he's quick to take your back, attacking and clinging like a damn monkey. I especially like wrestling with him because his speed helps to fine-tune my own skills, if they're ever needed in the field.

Come lunchtime, we're all drenched in sweat and panting, chugging water as if it's the sweetest nectar we've ever tasted. The sounds of heels clicking against the concrete floor draw our attention toward the door to see Phoebe striding up to us.

"I'm going to order some lunch. Do y'all want anything?" she asks softly.

Since the day I met her, I don't think I've ever heard that woman shout. I don't even think she can, even if her life depended on it. That's just who she is. Soft-spoken, kind, with one of the biggest hearts I know.

"I'm good, thanks. I plan on heading out." I take another drink of water. "I want to check in on Addi."

She nods and turns towards Boss and Einstein. Boss gives her the same answer I did, wanting to check in on Serenity.

"I'll have whatever you have," Einstein says before wiping his clean-shaven face free of sweat with his shirt, causing his pale abs and a dark patch of hair that circles his navel and disappears beneath the waistband of his workout shorts to be on display.

I don't miss the way her grey eyes dip briefly to his exposed torso before she drops them to the floor. I shake my head and laugh quietly to myself. *She's got it bad.*

"I'm thinking Asian food?" she says.

"Sounds good to me." Einstein drops his shirt before taking a drink of water.

Phoebe gives a small nod, turns on a black heel, and exits the room. I turn to find the evil genius's deep blue gaze glued to her retreating form. When she's no longer in sight, he turns toward us. Both Boss and I arch a brow in question at him.

"What?" He shrugs before running a hand with nails topped in lime green polish through his long raven hair that's normally contained in a grey beanie. The reason as to why he paints them is still a mystery. Boss and I continue to stare at him, silently communicating our response. "Fuck off," he groans, turns on his heel, and heads toward the locker room to shower and change.

I shake my head and turn toward Boss, finding him doing the same. "How's Renny holding up?"

"As good as can be right now," Boss blows out a breath. "She's been having nightmares. Not every night, but enough to make me want to resurrect that fucker so I can kill him slowly for what he did to both her and Addi." I huff in agreement. "How's Addi? Is she settling in alright?"

Boss's ice-blue and hazel gaze meets mine as concern fills them.

"I think so. She's been having nightmares as well. Nearly gave me a heart attack when she screamed bloody murder in her sleep the other night." Boss mutters a string of curses beneath his breath that I can't quite make out. Though with my vivid imagination, they aren't hard to guess. "It'll take some time, but at least I'm getting her to eat again."

His brows pinch together, causing the scar that bisects his left brow to be more prominent. He cocks his head, so I elaborate.

"The day we came back, she confessed that it had been roughly two days since she'd eaten. She'd said after everything went down, she'd lost her appetite. But because I'm a fucking badass chef, I have her eating properly again."

Boss's roaring laughter echoes throughout the gym. "Did she say that?"

"She didn't have to. Asking for seconds is a pretty good indicator." I laugh. "Well, I better get going. I wasn't there to make sure she ate breakfast, so I've got to make sure she eats some lunch."

"Sweeney." My name is a warning on his lips.

"Don't worry, Big Daddy." I give him a sly grin and hold up my hands in defense. "I'm being a good boy and keeping my hands to myself."

Except for the last two mornings, when I've woken up spooning her succulent body, but I keep that juicy bit of information to myself. He flips a middle finger to me, and I pretend to catch it and touch it to my heart. He laughs, shakes his head, and begins to gather his things to leave.

I pull into my driveway and park my bike in the garage before closing the metal door and walking into my house. My steps falter when I find it quiet. Too quiet.

"Honey, I'm home," I call out in a lighthearted tone as I set my keys in the glass bowl by the door and kick my shoes off in the closet. When there's no answer, I call out again. "Addi?"

I walk down the hall and enter the living room, scanning the space. She's nowhere to be found. It's noon. She can't still be asleep, can she?

"Addison!" I shout with slight panic in my voice.

I take the stairs three at a time and head straight for her room. Her door is closed, so I tap my knuckles against the wood. "Addi?"

"Come in," she calls out.

Her words are full of pain, and my stomach drops to my ass, my heart aches, and I throw the door open, hoping she's not hurt. The drapes are closed, keeping the room dark, and she's lying atop the covers in a fetal position. I'm across the room in three long strides as I stop beside the bed and start to scan her for injuries.

"What's wrong?" My gaze snags on her midsection, where she's clutching what looks to be a heating pad against her stomach.

"I was born a woman." She tries to laugh, but then groans in pain as if the movement hurts.

My brows furrow together, not catching her meaning.

"I happen to like the fact that you were born a woman." I force my tone to stay light despite my rising anxiety.

"Well, you don't have to suffer through bleeding for a week straight every month."

Ah, now I understand. Growing up around my mother and sister, I'm no stranger to the ins and outs of a woman's menstrual cycle.

I gently perch on the end of the bed, careful not to jostle her too much. "Are your periods normally this painful?"

"They've always been painful. Most of the time they're manageable with some Midol, but times like these…" She winces and takes a deep breath before continuing. On instinct, I begin to rub small circles across her lower back, remembering that's where the women in my life always said hurt the most during that time. "It leaves me stuck in bed for a day or two."

Women don't get enough credit for all the crap their bodies put them through. They deserve a damn medal for dealing with this. Not to mention childbirth. I stifle a shiver at the thought of the pain they go through. I know I couldn't do it.

"I'll be right back," I say and leave before she has a chance to question me.

After a quick run to the gas station around the corner, I race back upstairs and enter my bedroom. I take a five-second shower, just enough to wash the sweat from my body, and throw on some comfy clothes. I unplug the flatscreen TV that sits atop my dresser and bring it and the sacks into Addi's room.

"What are you doing?" Her voice is weak, and she attempts to laugh, only to wince.

"I don't know about you, but I need to know what happens in season two of *Dating Naked*." I set the TV down atop her dresser and plug it in. "I saw previews and the drama sounds pretty damn juicy."

I grab the sacks and the remote and gently settle atop the mattress next to her, my back propped up against the headboard. Addi takes a deep breath and rolls to her other side so she's facing me and can see the TV. She winces at the movement, and I help her untangle the cord to her heating pad and help her resettle it against her stomach.

She arches her brow. "What's in the sacks?"

"Chocolate." I grin down at her. "Lots of chocolate. And snacks."

Her dark eyes brighten, and a grin pulls at the lips I've wanted to kiss since the first day I met her. For the rest of the day, we lay there in bed snacking and binging our show, making comments and voicing our opinions on who we think will end up with whom. Honestly, I couldn't think of a better way to spend my day.

Chapter 9
ADDISON

"Hey, Renny!" I greet from the booth I secured for our dinner date.

For the last four years since meeting at our job at MoneyFirst Bank, Serenity and I have gone out for a girl's dinner almost every Friday to gossip, eat some good food, and have a few drinks. This is our first time back to a normal routine since my wedding day and the horrific events that followed. It's only been three weeks, but it feels as if a year has passed since I've seen my best friend.

"Hey, girl!" Serenity laughs and takes a seat across from me. "You seem like you're doing better."

"Way better! I mean, I still have bad moments, but those are growing fewer with each passing day. I feel like I'm starting to feel like the old me again. Slowly but surely." I answer and take a sip from my glass of wine.

I still have nightmares, but those are becoming less frequent and less severe. After my second night at Grayson's and testing out my theory, we agreed to sleep separately the following night to prove whether the experiment was successful or not. He had to wake me out of a horrific night terror. My throat was raw, and I knew I'd been screaming. My pajamas had clung to me from the sweat coating my body, and I was forced to shower and adorn fresh clothes before I attempted to go back to sleep.

After a long discussion, we agreed to test the theory a few more nights. Each passing morning, we woke and found that neither of us had had a bad dream all night. So, we tossed ideas around and settled on one that had me nervous but willing. We've been sleeping in the same bed each night since. Only sleeping! Nothing remotely sexual has happened. I'm still nowhere near ready for that. And even if I was, who's to say Grayson would do anything with me?

I also reached out to a therapist and have gone to a handful of sessions already. Our first session was the worst, having to tell and relive the horrible events that followed my wedding day. I know I still have a long way to go, but after each session, I feel a little lighter and a fraction closer to the old me again.

I've been back at work for two weeks now. The first day, I knew was going to be the hardest. All my coworkers knew I'd left for my honeymoon, so I did a lot of mental preparation for the awkward conversations I knew would come about why I wasn't wearing a ring anymore. But to my surprise, not one person said a single thing. Don't get me wrong, people stared at my now naked finger, but no one asked what happened.

Without asking, I knew Serenity had spoken with the entire staff about leaving me alone. I couldn't have been more thankful for my best friend. Knowing that she went through it with me and suffered right alongside me, but looked out for me in the end, made my heart ache. Not with agonizing pain that's growing fainter by the day, but with pride and love.

"I'm so glad to hear that." Serenity's smile is brighter than the sun, causing her green eyes to sparkle as she takes a sip from her glass of wine.

"So, how have you been?"

"Besides dealing with legal crap, I've been great. Hunter is amazing and living with him is like a dream that I never want to wake up from." A small blush tints her olive cheeks. "A part of me doesn't want to find my own place anymore."

Another item on the ever-growing list of things I'll forever be grateful for about my best friend is the fact that she took care of all of Jack's legal stuff. He'd left everything to Serenity in his will, and I meant it when I told her I wanted nothing. So, these last few weeks she's been selling everything he owned and handling his bank accounts.

"Then don't." I take another sip and wiggle my brows suggestively.

"Don't let Hunter hear you say that. He would have you trying to convince me to stay at his place." Serenity laughs fully. "How's living with Sweeney?"

I can feel a slight blush start to heat my cheeks. "Honestly, it's been great."

"If he has been anything less than a gentleman, tell me, and I'll kick his ass for you."

"No, he's been wonderful. I have my own room and bathroom at his place. He gives me space when I need it. He helps me through panic attacks, which are getting better by the way. He makes me laugh when I feel like crying, and he cooks for me."

He sleeps next to me each night, which keeps the nightmares at bay. Most of the time. When he's away for work, and I'm alone, those nights are terrible, and I find myself looking forward to his return. When he came home and learned I was on my period and in severe pain, he went beyond any expectation and took care of me, lying in bed with me all day watching TV.

I nearly cried at his compassionate and caring side, but I knew that my hormones were to blame. Never once had Jack done anything like that in our years of dating when I got my period. He wasn't an asshole by any means. He'd bring me pain meds if I asked, make a run to the store if I ran out of tampons, and would even lie with me for a bit. But he never went that extra mile.

He never rubbed soothing circles or massaged the aches in my back away. Never brought me sweets or food of any kind, without me asking, because he thought it would make me feel better. And he sure as hell never spent the *entire* day in bed with me, taking my mind off my cramps while we binged trashy TV.

I'll never forget what Grayson has done and continues to do for me. It's another example on my never-ending list of how he's been so amazing in my healing journey.

"He also got me in touch with the lawyer who works for Red Sky Security and helped me get my marriage annulled." I release a deflated sigh. "It's as if it never happened."

Which, honestly, is one of the biggest blessings that I'll ever know. I held my emotions together long enough for us to get back to Grayson's truck, but the moment we were alone, I cried. A part of me was still mourning the loss of what I thought my and Jack's relationship was and the fiery end it came to. I cried with joy that I never had to take the psychopath's last name. I cried with sorrow that after years of devoting everything to a relationship, all I had to show for it in the end was a shattered heart. I cried in joy, as horrible as that might sound, that it was finally over. That the last tie I had to that piece of shit had been severed.

"How's the house search going?" Serenity inquires.

"Not so great." My shoulders slouch and I groan. "Every time I find a place that might work, Sweeney finds something wrong with it. Sometimes they're legit reasons, but other times it seems like he tries to find something wrong, so I have to stay there with him."

Despite all the good Grayson's done, I still need to find my own place. I knew from the start that living with him wasn't going to be permanent. My therapist has even hinted that soon I'll be ready to be on my own again.

"Then stay there with him for a while," she suggests. "From what you tell me, he's been helping tremendously with your healing process. Why not stay a while longer, until you're fully healed and ready to be on your own?"

"I don't know." I blow out a heavy breath. "Maybe you're right."

"Haven't you learned by now? I'm always right." She laughs and I join her. The sound of us both happy again warms my fractionally healed heart. "On to a more serious topic. I want you to have the money. Everything's been handled and dealt with, so you won't have to worry about anything except what you want to spend it on."

I know Serenity is trying hard to keep her voice light on such a touchy subject, but it doesn't stop the sickening feeling churning deep in my stomach.

"I can't do that, Renny. After what he did, you should take it."

How can I accept that money? Jack stalked her, terrorized her, violated her in unspeakable ways, and hurt her. She deserves it as much as she believes I do.

"Then let's split it, please. It's too much for one to have alone," Serenity counters. "You can leave it sitting in accounts to grow off interest for the rest of your life, or you can buy your dream house with it. It's totally up to you."

I pause for a moment, considering. He did both of us dirty, each in a unique way. What better way to say fuck you than to use his money to make ourselves happy while he burns in hell? At least I hope that's where he is. He deserves nothing less.

"Fine, half," I agree with a small smile. "How much was there anyway?"

The amount had never once crossed my mind.

"Just over six million." Her words nearly make me choke on my wine, and my chocolate gaze widens with surprise.

"Holy shit!" I shout. "And he gave me a hard time for buying new towels for the bathroom when I first moved in. Cheapskate." I shake my head and look toward my friend. We both pause and burst out laughing.

Serenity and I lost track of time, and night had fallen when I finally pulled my Dodge Challenger into Grayson's driveway. The knot in my stomach grows tighter as I grab the small rectangular box resting in my passenger seat, wrapped in dark red paper, and exit my car. The list of everything he's done for me seems to be forever growing, and I wanted to do something for him to show my appreciation.

I've been wracking my brain all week trying to come up with something I could get him, and as I was walking through the mall the other day, my vision was drawn to a particular shop, and I knew I'd found the winner. I would've given it to him that night when I got home, but he's been gone the last three days on a bodyguard assignment out on the west coast and wasn't due back until today.

It's been so quiet around the house without his wonderful humor and inappropriate jokes that never fail to make me laugh. I thought I'd never laugh again, but he seems persistent in drawing it out of me at least five times a day. And a part of me I like to keep pushing to the back of my mind looks forward to tonight because I know he'll be sleeping in bed next to me, and his presence, for reasons still mysterious to me, keeps my nightmares at bay. I haven't gotten much sleep these last few days, but I'll never tell him that.

The security system chimes quickly three times as I enter the front door and lock it behind me. I kick off my shoes and place them in the hall closet as I pad down the hallway and enter the kitchen. I can't stop the smile that tugs my face up when I see Grayson leaning against the kitchen counter, feet crossed at the ankles as he brings a beer to his full lips. He's dressed in pajama pants and a T-shirt that leaves nothing to the imagination of how muscular his torso truly is.

I quickly avert my gaze as I stow his gift behind my back, stop a few feet from him, and lean back against the island, facing him.

"Welcome home," I greet in a chipper voice.

Maybe too chipper, so I quietly clear my throat and take a calming breath. *Stupid nerves.* I truly hope he likes his gift.

"It's good to be home." He flashes me a dazzling smile that sends a small wave of butterflies through my stomach. I ignore them. Completely! His thick brow arches high as his honey vision drops down my front and back up again. "Planning on killing me with whatever's behind your back?"

I snort and roll my eyes. "If I wanted to kill you, I'd do it while you slept. Less of a struggle."

"Ah, smart woman." He nods approvingly and takes another swig of alcohol. I take a deep breath and extend the present toward him. He eyes it, his face scrunching in question. "What's that?"

"It's a gift." I wave it at him, signaling for him to take it. "For you."

"Oh!" His whisky eyes light up, and he beams like a child on Christmas morning. "It's neither my birthday nor Christmas. What's the occasion?"

He begins to tear the wrapping off quite eagerly, and I can't help but laugh.

"It's a thank-you gift." He tosses the torn-up wrapping paper haphazardly behind him, gaining a genuine laugh from me as he cocks his head to the side, so I elaborate further. "You've opened up your home to me, you've fed me, make sure I get enough sleep each night. You went above and beyond when I was laid up in bed in pain."

"All of which are just parts of being a decent human being that anyone should do." He chuckles lightly. "You didn't have to get me anything to show your thanks."

"You've done more for me in the last few weeks than..." I take a deep breath before continuing. "Than Jack ever did for me in the years we were together. You've been such a huge part of helping me heal, I try not to imagine where I would be right now if you hadn't helped the way you have and continue to do so." I meet his gaze, and my heart skips a beat. His face is schooled in a carefree mask, but I don't miss the intense emotions that swirl within his irises. "It's nothing too fancy." I nod toward the box and chuckle. "Just a little something to say thank you."

He's quiet for a moment as if numerous thoughts and emotions are causing confusion within before he drops his gaze to his hands and opens the lid to the rectangular box. I notice the way his eyes nearly double in size as he reaches slowly and removes a dagger the length of my forearm. The hilt is made of thick white bone with elegant swirls carved into it. The five-inch blade has a wave shape that features jagged, serrated teeth lining the backside. The silver gleams beneath the kitchen lights as he turns it over and inspects every inch of it.

"Do you like it?" My voice is apprehensive as I pick at the hem of my shirt and try hard not to bounce anxiously on my toes.

"Like it?" He whispers, and my heart drops, fearing the worst. "I fucking love it!"

I release a breath I didn't realize I was holding. "That one caught my eye, and I had to get it."

I knew when I saw the weapons shop that anything lying in the display case filled with an assortment of unique blades would do the trick. For unknown reasons, this man has a knife kink that I don't even try to begin to understand. There's a reason he was gifted his call sign based on Sweeney Todd.

"This is by far the best gift anyone has ever given me." He clears the hint of emotion from his throat and peers up at me with a breathtaking smile. "Thank you."

I watch as he sets the empty box atop the counter and begins to twirl the blade around in his hand. He tosses it from hand to hand, as if testing the weight before twirling it and then sending it flipping through the air. My breath hitches when I see him catch the tip of the blade between his finger and thumb effortlessly. Then he tosses it again and grips the handle tightly in a fist as he goes through a few slicing maneuvers as if he's fighting an invisible opponent.

Everything he does is hotter than it has any right to be. I've seen him work. He gave me the option to shield my eyes or see the real him as he dealt with the last criminal Jack hired to kill me. Though he was slicing up a human being, torturing and playing with him like a cat torments a mouse before they kill them, I was mesmerized by his movements. Grayson flowed with such grace, such beauty, each cut so exact and precise, that I couldn't help but be in awe. It's as if he were a swordsman who's been battling his entire life and has mastered the dance.

He straightens, approaches me, and places a soft kiss atop my head. I freeze and my heart rate skyrockets to an alarming rate. He steps back, allowing a few feet to separate us again before he speaks.

"I didn't offer to help you in hopes of being rewarded with gifts, Addi. I don't ever want you to feel as if you owe me for anything. Do you understand?"

I nod because I don't trust my voice, knowing it will crack with the emotions constricting my throat.

"Don't get me wrong, I love gifts as much as the next person. Especially the pointy kind." He grins, wiggles his brows mischievously, and flips the blade one more time, catching it by the hilt. "I offered to help because I knew you needed a friend. I don't care if it takes five years before you're fully ready to move on and be out on your own again. I'm here for every minute of it with no expectations of repayment."

"I understand." I clear my throat and laugh. "Though, if I want to get you a gift, there's nothing you can do to stop me."

"I wouldn't dream of it." He flashes me a smile before I turn and head upstairs to shower before bed.

Chapter 10

ADDISON

"We don't have to go out tonight if you don't want to." Grayson tries to give me an out for the fourth time, and like all the times before, I politely decline.

"No, it's ok." I inhale slowly, willing calm to settle in. "I want to go. Halloween is one of my favorite holidays."

All the guys from Red Sky Security, Phoebe, Serenity, and myself are meeting up at a farm twenty minutes outside the city. Each year, the owners decorate it for the spooky season, offering haunted trail rides, a massive corn maze where monsters and masked scarers wield weapons and chase frightened attendees through the stalks, pumpkin carving, one of the top-rated haunted houses in the state constructed within one of the numerous large barns, and many more activities.

They also offer killer food—no pun intended—that you can only find at hole-in-the-wall places and an amazing alcohol tent with a selection of the cheapest beers around. People from all over the country visit Oklahoma just to experience one of the most terrifying thriller parks in the nation.

Though this is my favorite time of the year, I'm apprehensive because this is the first social outing I'll be attending since the ugly events following my wedding. The first social outings I'll be attending as a single woman, without Jack by my side.

Not that I want that psychotic piece of shit anywhere near me. I'd be tempted to trip him in the corn maze and stand by with a smile on my face while someone dressed as Leatherface gives him a makeover with their chainsaw. That thought alone already has me smiling and wishing I could make it a reality.

I pull the sleeve of my sweater down over my hands and close the fabric in my fists, loving the way the soft material helps to calm my racing anxiety.

"Ok." He holds the passenger door of his Toyota Tacoma open for me, and I climb in. "But if you want to leave at any time, no questions asked, just tell me."

"Alright then, what's the safeword?" I inquire playfully, though my nerves can easily be heard in my tone.

His vision narrows, and a wicked grin slowly turns up his full lips. "I don't do safewords, sweetheart." Wings erupt in my stomach that have nothing to do with my apprehension, but before I can linger on the feeling, he continues. "When you're ready to leave, simply hold my hand and give it three quick squeezes."

Sounds simple and easy enough to remember.

"Deal." I give him as brave a smile as I can muster.

Nearly half an hour later, due to traffic, we're pulling down a dirt road and parking in a massive field that the owners transformed into a makeshift parking lot for the Halloween season. There's a nip in the air, causing me to wrap my arms around my middle and walk a bit closer to Grayson as we weave through the parking lot toward the entrance where we've agreed to meet everyone.

It was a good call on the thick wool. I feared I'd be sweating halfway through the night, but the breath I see misting in front of me with each exhale now has me fearing my nipples will slice through my very expensive bra from the cold. I'm brought out of my thoughts as we approach a group of very tall, very intimidating-looking men who tower over Serenity and Phoebe, who are huddled close together in hopes of staying warm.

After greetings are made, Fuse speaks as he shoves his hands in the front pockets of his jeans. "Beer first, then we'll go from there."

"Best plan you've ever suggested." Doc claps him on the shoulder and beams a pearly white smile that pops against his beautiful bronzed skin.

We file through a line that leads us to an old-fashioned ticket booth. After paying the entry fee and passing through security, where they make sure we're not concealing any weapons, Hunter and Serenity, hands clasped together, lead the way. His massive height makes it easy to follow as we weave through a crowd of people. Some have their heads thrown back with laughter, some clutch steaming cups of hot chocolate, others chow down on food as they move from tent to tent, checking out the various merchandise, crafts, and apparel for sale.

Halloween-themed music plays through loudspeakers set up in various spots around the main area. I smile when I see half of the patrons dressed in various costumes, some with spooky or elaborate face paint and colorful wigs. Others chose to dress warmly in sweaters or flannels, and pants with earmuffs or beanies shielding their ears from the dropping temperature.

My stomach growls as the aroma of delicious BBQ hits me, causing my head to swivel in hopes of locating it. I'll make the suggestion of obtaining food after we all get drinks. The faint sounds of screams and chainsaws occasionally drown out the music from the direction of the corn maze, and strobe lights flash off toward a barn in the back where the haunted house lies within.

With each step that carries me further into the park, I feel my anxiety slowly begin to relax. Maybe it's the atmosphere putting me at ease. Maybe it's because I'm in a group with five very dangerous men, some ex-military, but all of whom could confidently take a life in a matter of seconds without batting an eye. Maybe it's because Grayson stays close to my side the entire time, his presence enveloping me in a promise of absolute security. Or maybe it's a combination of all three. Whichever reason it is, I'm thankful for it.

We all chat as we wait in line at the beer tent, inching closer to the counter with each passing minute. When we finally reach the front, Grayson orders us both a large cup of spiked hot apple cider. I sigh in relief at the first sip, loving the warmth that spreads through my chest and begins to heat me from the inside out.

"The security here is a joke." Hunter shakes his head in disappointment as we all gather outside the tent with our drinks clutched tightly in our grasps, Serenity clinging desperately to his side for warmth.

"Why?" Phoebe's voice pitches as her pale grey eyes dart around the chaotic crowd behind her colorful rimmed glasses. She's dressed in a wool sweater covered with tiny candy corns and a pair of bell-bottom jeans. I smile when I observe the knitted candy corn beanie that helps to protect her ears from the cold, topped with a fuzzy pom-pom. Only she'd be able to pull off something that innocent and adorable. "Do you see something?"

"Relax, Blue." Doc chuckles lightly, picking up on her rising fear of possible danger, and nudges her playfully with his elbow.

"He means because we're all packing, and they were none the wiser." Fuse elaborates with a smile as he runs his hand over his neatly trimmed reddish-brown beard.

Phoebe peers around the group, her vision slightly widened with shock. I'm right there with her, silently wondering what kind of weapon each man is carrying. And where?

"All of you?" Her voice squeaks with nerves.

"A knife tucked in my right boot." Fuse shoots her a wink.

"A pistol holstered behind my back and a knife in my right boot," Doc adds with a satisfied grin.

Hunter nods in agreement. "A blade sheathed in each boot."

I shift my gaze to Grayson, who's cheesing like an idiot. "Six blades."

I nearly choke on my drink, trying to figure out all the hiding places he could stash them on his body. He's dressed casually in jeans and a thick black and grey flannel.

"Is that even physically possible?" Serenity questions hesitantly, her mossy eyes wide as she scans his large frame.

"That's me packing light." Grayson laughs.

Fuse, Einstein, Doc, and Hunter join in, shaking their heads because they know Grayson's not joking. I can't help but join them. *I'm living with a psychopath. Smart move, Addi.* The group's vision shifts to Einstein, the last to speak up. He stands next to Phoebe, dressed in a black hoodie with a skeleton hand over his left pec, the middle finger sticking straight up. His raven hair wings out beneath a well-loved grey beanie.

"A gun," he pats at his right front hip, "and a blade in my left boot."

Though the sun has long since set and they've got lights illuminating the area, I don't miss the slight blush that colors Phoebe's creamy cheeks. She tries to hide it by taking a long, slow swig of her drink, but I catch it. Judging by the arch of Hunter's brows, he catches it too, but we keep our comments to ourselves.

"Well," I clear my throat, drawing seven pairs of eyes my way, "now that we're all in possession of alcohol and armed for battle, I vote we follow the smell of that delicious BBQ next."

After everyone agrees, we move through the crowd and secure food. The pulled pork sandwich was quite literally the best food I've ever had in my life. And from the way our group didn't utter a single word as we ate, it's safe to say that everyone would agree with me. With our bellies full and alcohol warming our blood, we head straight toward the haunted house.

After waiting in line for about twenty minutes, our group finally enters, and I find myself clinging to Grayson's shirt like it's my lifeline as I bury my face into his side. I can feel his body shake with laughter each time I get jump-scared, and a shriek leaves my lips, but he keeps an arm draped casually around my waist.

We twist and turn around corners where people dressed as monsters, creepy dolls, or scary clowns wait to scare us and pass through numerous gruesome scenes. One has a child sitting on the floor, brushing a doll's hair. I couldn't place it, but something was unsettling about the way she sang her nursery rhymes. Her words were slow and her voice eerie, causing goosebumps to pebble my skin and the hair on the back of my neck to rise. Another room had a man lying on a metal table of a morgue, with a mortician cutting into his chest cavity. Only, the man wasn't dead.

His screams of agony had my skin crawling, and I may have walked a bit faster toward the exit that would take us into yet another creepy scene. Strobe lights obstruct our vision, and fog machines conceal everything below our ankles. My heart is racing, and I feel as if I'll lose my voice tomorrow by the time we finally reach the exit and the cold night air washes over my heated skin.

I notice Phoebe step away from Einstein's side. She was hiding behind him like I was with Grayson, and Serenity was with Hunter.

"Woooo!" Grayson's loud voice booms through the quiet around us as we loop around the building toward the crowd again. "Who's up for round two?"

"You're a glutton for punishment." Fuse laughs.

"You fucking know it!" Grayson agrees with a wicked grin.

Instead of entering the haunted barn again, we continue down a dirt path that will take us to the corn maze. Screams, some faint while others sound right next to us, fill my ears, and a giddy anticipation bubbles within me. I may have had my head buried in Grayson's shirt most of the time in the haunted house, but I loved every minute of it. My cheeks hurt from smiling so much, and I'm so glad I decided to join them tonight. We come to a stop at the line that leads to the entrance of the maze.

"I hear you have to sign a waiver before entering," Serenity comments.

"Really?" Doc's brows furrow. "Why?"

Fuse laughs and points his thumb over his shoulder. "They probably want to make sure no one tries to sue them after suffering a heart attack in there."

We move up in line and Einstein speaks next, correcting us. "Actually, you have to sign a waiver because the scarers are allowed to put their hands on you if they find and catch you."

I beg your finest fucking pardon? We all stare at him in shocked silence.

"What?" I whisper in horror.

"Yeah." He laughs. "They have traps set up throughout the maze where, if they catch you, they can carry you off and lock you down for five minutes. Cuff you to chairs, lock you in an oversized, less stabby iron maiden, strap you to a gurney, shit like that."

"What the fuck?" Serenity gasps in complete terror.

"It's alright." Einstein laughs again. "It's completely safe. They don't hit. They can only carry. You aren't allowed to hit either. If you're caught, you have to go with them until your five-minute timeout is over. Then they release you to continue the maze. Their weapons are fake, minus the chainsaws, but they've removed the chains. If you're shut inside something, it's passed rigorous safety inspections to make sure there's enough airflow and no one is harmed. That's why they have you sign the waiver. They don't want someone suing them because they're claustrophobic and they want your word that you won't swing at their scarers."

"I'm sorry, but if some dude in face paint tries to carry me off, I'm swinging." Doc scoffs, and Hunter nods in agreement.

"Same." Fuse shakes his head. "It'll be lights out for them."

"I'd love to see them try to carry my large, heavy ass." Grayson laughs.

"I don't want to add to the bad news," Phoebe speaks up as she points toward the entrance, and we all shift our gaze. "They're patting everyone down before they enter the maze. More thoroughly than security did at the front."

"They'll surely find y'all's weapons." My shoulders drop, fearing we won't get to experience the maze that brings people in from across the country.

Though the thought of getting caught and trapped for five minutes each time does sound a bit scary, I know there's no way I'd get hurt. Like Einstein said, they've taken every safety precaution they could think of, which helps to ease my anxiety. I watch as Serenity's shoulders drop too, most likely thinking the same things I am.

"If you ladies want to go in, that's up to you." Hunter shifts his gaze between Serenity, Phoebe, and me. "We'll wait for y'all at the exit."

Serenity claps her hands together and tucks them beneath her chin, a bright smile blossoming across her face. "Really?"

"But you three have to stick together." His ice-blue and hazel gaze skims over the three of us.

Phoebe, Serenity, and I share glances. A silent conversation happens between us as looks of both apprehension and anticipation cross our faces. Excitement and curiosity win out in the end, and we all nod in confirmation. With that, the men stay with us as we reach the front of the line, sign the waivers, and bid the men farewell. After we're each patted down and cleared, we enter the maze and stay close together with me in the lead, Serenity following behind, and Phoebe bringing up the rear.

Chapter 11

ADDISON

The stalks of corn tower over our heads, standing close to eight or nine feet high, all varying in shades of brown and tan. Harvesting season was months ago, but they'll wait until November to bale the stalks, giving them the perfect environment for a haunted maze. The sound of the crowd back in the main area of the farm dies down the deeper we move. Shop lights are stationed every so often throughout, enough to light our way but still dim enough to cast spooky shadows and have us fearing someone's about to jump out and get us any second.

A woman's high-pitched scream sounds from somewhere to our right, followed by a man's deep, menacing laugh, causing my heart to jump right up my damn throat.

"Which way should we go?" I whisper over my shoulder as we approach a dead end that either branches off right or left. I'm unsure if any scarers are close by, and I'm not about to alert them of our presence.

"Uh… left?" Serenity suggests.

I peer around the corner of wilted stalks, making sure the coast is clear before fully committing. My heart is jackhammering in my chest at the unknown, at the possibility of a monster spotting us. The thought of being chased by masked people or creatures should warn anyone away, but that's what Halloween is all about: pushing your limits and forcing yourself into unnerving situations because the adrenaline that floods your veins is like morphine. Addicting.

When I see we're alone, we round the corner and curve around a slight bend to the right. We try to keep our steps light, but our shoes crunch beneath the dirt path and dead leaves.

"Is it bad that being chased by a masked man is kind of… intriguing?"

Phoebe's soft voice has Serenity and I both stopping mid-step. We turn and pin her with a look, our brows hiked high in a combination of surprise and disbelief. A deep apple-red heats her creamy cheeks, and I know it has nothing to do with the cold.

"What?" Phoebe shrugs and squeaks out the question.

"Huh." I huff a laugh. "It really is the quiet ones who're the freakiest." I give her a bright, knowing grin and wiggle my dark brows.

"Damn, girl." Serenity snickers quietly. "I didn't know you were into that kind of stuff."

That only serves to deepen Phoebe's embarrassment.

"I didn't… I mean…" She fumbles over her words.

I quickly reassure her with a smile. "We're just giving you shit."

"Actually…" Serenity cocks her head and places her finger against her chin. "The thought of Hunter chasing me, all burly and masked, with threats of devilish sin when he catches me does sound pretty damn fun."

I, on the other hand, stifle a shiver that tries to creep down my spine. I've already experienced that. Two men, chasing me through the woods, forcing me to run as I'd never run before, and unable to look back for fear of tripping. I knew what they wanted to do to me when they finally caught me. Thankfully, Grayson caught up to us and stopped them before things progressed too far.

"No, thanks. I'll pass." I shake my head and continue forward, my steps slow and sure.

I feel Serenity loosen her grip on my sweater as she runs a soothing hand across my back, knowing she guessed exactly what I was thinking. That I was remembering something that happened just a month ago. Emotions clog my throat and constrict my heart like a vise at the love I have for my sister. We come to another stop when we can either go left, right, or continue moving straight.

I keep my voice hushed. "Now where?"

"Straight?" Serenity offers.

I pick up my foot to start walking again, only to freeze. A massive brick wall of a man dressed as Jason Voorhees comes into view ahead of us. His large hand grips a massive machete with red smeared across the fake blade. He cocks his head to the side, and I know all three of us collectively stop breathing.

"How about we go right?" Phoebe offers in a shaky whisper.

"Good call." I nod, and a heartbeat later, I'm turning us off that path and onto a new one.

I quicken our pace just a bit to put a little distance between us and the man wearing a bloodied hockey mask. We make another immediate right and stay straight for a few feet before turning left.

While rounding the corner, I smack right into something hard, causing me to yelp in surprise as Serenity bumps into my back.

We all take a step back and peer up to see a tall, lanky man with his face painted white with blue triangles around his dark eyes. The red around his mouth makes his smile appear unsettlingly large, and his wig of bright orange hair sticks out in all directions as if he were just electrocuted. A massive axe is clutched in one hand, and his clown suit is ripped in places and smeared with dark red stains.

His warning is deep as he grins wickedly at us. "Run."

You don't have to tell us twice. Instantly, we pivot so Phoebe is in the lead, and take off running at full speed. The sounds of heavy footsteps thudding into the ground behind me are confirmation enough that the killer clown is, in fact, chasing us. And he's fucking close.

"Go! Go! Go!" I shout, urging my friends to run faster.

A smile spreads across my face at the thrill, and jolts of adrenaline have my body tingling. This is what Halloween is all about, and I'm fucking here for it. All day, every day. Phoebe makes a quick right, then an immediate left, and I hear the clown's heavy footsteps begin to slowly fade. He could've caught us so easily, but that takes all the fun out of the game. The chase is what gives people the thrill, and he knows how to do his job in a way that will give us the most out of this experience.

You chase a few people here and there, some longer than others, taunting them. Then, eventually, you capture an unlucky few and repeat the process, all night. It's all a game, and they're masters at their craft. I spare a glance, and as I thought, the clown is no longer behind us.

Looking back caused my steps to slow enough to put space between Serenity and me. When I peer forward again, I see her and Phoebe round a bend to our left, not five feet ahead of me. Just as I reach the bend, a shirtless man with red smeared across his muscular torso steps into my path, and I'm forced to skid to a stop.

My chest is heaving as I try to catch my breath. His dark pants have patches sewn all over them, and his face is painted to resemble a scarecrow. How he's able to be shirtless in this cold is beyond me. I go to turn and run back the way we came, but his arm on my bicep stops me.

"Where do you think you're going?" His deep voice is filled with mirth and slices through the quiet night air.

I point with my free hand in the direction we came. "Um… back that way?"

I know it's useless, but I try to crack a joke. Maybe he'll laugh and agree that my sense of humor is cause to let me go so I can catch back up to my friends. My joke has only half its intended effect. He laughs but doesn't let me go. His grip on me is gentle but firm, and I know that if I were to yank my arm away, he'd let go.

However, that's not how this works. I was caught, which means I have to be locked in a timeout of sorts for the next five minutes. The thought of having to finish this maze on my own has my mouth going dry, but it'll be alright. Maybe my friends will wait close by, so when my time is done and I'm freed, we can continue together.

"Nice try." He laughs and shakes his head. "But that won't work on me."

Without warning, he bends down, pulls me over his shoulder, and stands again as if I weigh as much as a small child.

"Well, this is humiliating…" I prop my elbows against his back and rest my chin in my hands. A strong arm wraps around the back of my thighs, securing me in place as he starts walking in the opposite direction Serenity and Phoebe ran.

A few seconds later, I see their heads pop out from around a stalk, and I can't stop the smile that spreads across my face. I knew they'd wait for me. I watch as they slowly start to trail behind us, making sure to keep quiet so they don't get caught too. They'll hide close by, and once my five minutes are up, we'll be able to continue together.

We turn, and I peer around to see exactly how I'll be spending the next few minutes. My mind races to recall all the scenarios Einstein had listed while we waited in line. But what I see has the blood draining from my face, and true panic starts to settle in. About twenty feet ahead of us is an old, beat-up, rusted car with its rear end sticking out onto the dirt path.

The car isn't the problem. It's the open trunk that has the spiced apple cider souring my stomach, making my dinner want to reappear, and my hands going clammy. One second, I'm in a corn maze with my friends, tossed over the shoulder of a scarecrow and having a blast, and the next, I'm back in Hawaii, tossed over Baldy's shoulder as he walks toward the open trunk of a car that will take me into the woods where I'll be forced to run for my life as two criminals try to rape and murder me.

My fight or flight instinct kicks in, and I begin to squirm against my capture. "No! Please don't put me in there! Let me go!"

I feel him shake with laughter beneath me, but he doesn't listen. I begin to pound my fists into his back, but before I know it, I'm tossed into the trunk, the air being stolen from my lungs as I land with a hard thud. I try to scream, to plead with him to let me go, but no sounds come out. I don't see a shirtless scarecrow standing before me. Instead, it's Baldy with his large hand resting atop the trunk door, a sinister smile across his beefy face, and his black eyes peering down at me, promising that I won't like what's about to come, but he will.

"I'll be back in five minutes." He gives me a wicked smile before he shuts the lid and darkness settles around me.

I try again to call out, but the only sound that escapes is a small, choked whimper. With the help of Grayson and my therapist, my panic attacks have been getting better, but the one now consuming my mind and body is like none I've ever experienced before. I try to calm my breathing, but it's futile, and I'm clutching at my chest as I gasp, trying to take in as much oxygen as I can.

Thankfully, there are numerous large holes in the side of the trunk, allowing plenty of airflow and a bit of light to filter through the cramped space. My eyes immediately dart up to where the trunk release should be, but it's bare, and a second whimper escapes.

I've never been claustrophobic. I could crawl under a bed, hide in a closet, ride an elevator, and be perfectly fine. Even after everything that happened after my wedding and all I endured, I still wasn't claustrophobic because we rode in an elevator to the lawyer's office, and I was completely fine.

But... I haven't been in a trunk since...

I can't breathe, can't think. With no possible way to escape on my own, all I can do is pull my knees to my chest as warm tears begin to flow down my cheeks and tremors begin to shake my body.

Chapter 12
SWEENEY

My brothers and I watch as the women enter the corn maze, and we don't move until they disappear from our sight. We begin walking the perimeter before rounding to the back and coming to a stop at a sign that signals the exit.

"How long do you think it will take them?" Doc questions as he shoves his hands into the pockets of his jeans, in an attempt to keep them warm.

"No idea." Fuse shrugs.

"As long as they don't get separated, I'm sure they'll be out in no time," Boss offers.

"They're together," Einstein states casually, drawing all eyes to him.

He's peering down at his phone, one hand tucked into his pants pocket. When we don't answer, he brings his head up, and his deep sapphire gaze takes in all our confused expressions. Then, he holds up his phone toward us. The screen shows what appears to be an aerial view of… a fucking maze with three blinking pins that move at a slow but steady pace through the paths.

Doc points to the screen. "Dude, is that…"

"That's fucking creepy…" I trail off as my vision shifts from the phone back to Einstein.

He shrugs casually. "What? Did you really think I wouldn't be keeping an eye on them?" He snorts. "I'm always watching, remember?"

"Einstein, do we need to have another talk about privacy?" Boss's deep voice drawls through the quiet air as he pinches the bridge of his nose.

"No," Einstein answers innocently before flashing a dazzling smile. "I remember everything from our previous talks."

"Fucking hell…" Fuse can't help but laugh, and we all join in.

Einstein turns the phone back to himself and we all nonchalantly take a step closer as we try to watch the screen. Creases form across his forehead in amusement and he chuckles to himself as he extends the phone to a better position for us all to watch.

Minutes tick by as we watch the three blinking dots slowly make their way deeper into the maze. We comment when we notice them make a wrong turn, as if they can hear us, but none of us can tear our eyes away from the screen. My pulse shoots up when the dots begin to move fast down a row, signaling that the women must be running.

I should've gone in there with Addi. What the hell was I thinking, letting her go into a place like that alone? A place where the scarers are allowed to chase you and haul you away to be restrained for minutes at a time until you eventually find the exit. I start to give myself an internal lecture, but stop when I remember what Einstein said.

It's as safe as it can be. The weapons are fake, and they've taken every safety precaution they could think of while guests are being restrained once caught. She'll be alright. It's all pure Halloween fun.

Boss points to the screen at the last pin. "Why did that one stop?"

His words bring me back to the present, and I narrow my vision as I watch the first two dots keep moving at a quickened pace. The one left behind stays there for what feels like minutes when in reality, it was merely a matter of seconds.

"It's moving again," Doc announces as if we aren't all watching the same thing.

I comment next. "It's going the wrong way."

That pin is now moving away from the other two.

"One of the girls must've gotten caught," Einstein offers, and we all peer up to glare at him.

He best be fucking joking. However, I know he's right when I notice the first two dots stop and begin moving slowly in the opposite direction, following the third dot. *Good, they're sticking together.* A satisfied smile crosses my face, but it drops when the third dot stops moving. The other two halt as well, a bit away, as if watching from a distance.

Who got caught? How are they being restrained right now? Are they chained to a chair? Strapped to a gurney? Locked in a massive coffin? Or was it an iron maiden? I can't fucking remember. I try to recall all the ways the evil genius told us earlier, but it's useless. However they're captured, I know they'll be alright. He said the owners prided themselves on keeping it completely safe for the guests.

The minutes tick by, and once five have passed, deep creases form between our brows when we notice the pins don't move. Well, the first two did, coming to a stop right next to the one that was captured, but they don't continue through the maze. Did the scarer not release them? Are they all captured now?

Einstein pulls my next words straight from my brain. "What the hell is going on?"

A phone rings, and we all avert our gaze from the screen to watch as Boss withdraws his cell phone from his jeans and answers it, putting it on speakerphone for us all to hear.

"Angel, what's wrong?" His words are calm, but I've known him long enough to hear the unease hiding behind them.

"It's Addi." Serenity's panicked words have my heart stopping in my chest.

I'm unable to keep from speaking up, "What the fuck do you mean? Is she hurt?"

Blood roars in my ears, and I return to internally berating myself for allowing her to go into the maze without me. I'm such a damn idiot. *I swear if anything's happened to her, I'll—* My thoughts are cut off by Serenity's answer.

"She got caught by some scarecrow guy. She was fine at first. We watched as he carried her off down the path." I begin to see red at the mention that another man not only had his hands on her but also carried her. Before I'm able to visualize my blades tasting his blood, she continues. "Addi was fine at first, but when she saw where she would be spending the next five minutes, she began to freak out. She started kicking and hitting the guy, begging him to put her down."

Yep, I'm going to murder that scarecrow.

"And he didn't fucking release her?" Fuse's rage can easily be heard in every word he grits out through a clenched jaw.

"No, he said he thought it was all an act, her way of playing along to make the experience more real. If he knew it was true panic that she was experiencing, he said he would've let her go right away. But before Addi could go on, he tossed her into the trunk of an old car and shut the lid."

Oh no…

"What? Is she claustrophobic or something?" Doc's question is sincere and laced with worry.

"No," Boss clips. "Back in Hawaii, the two criminals hired to kill her had thrown her in a trunk and driven her into the woods."

My brothers knew the basics of everything that happened last month after Addi's wedding, but they didn't know the details, minus Einstein. Somehow, the little genius always knows everything. Neither Boss nor I thought it was important to spare details that were personal to the women. If they wanted the men to know, they would tell them their full stories. If they didn't, Boss and I planned to take them to our graves.

"Oh shit," both Fuse and Doc say in unison.

They aren't strangers to trauma and PTSD. None of us are. We all know just how ugly it can be and how it can sink its claws deep into your mind and take you back to a past time. Always at the most inconvenient moments too.

"We thought she was fine. We didn't hear her scream or call out or anything," Phoebe adds from the other end of the call, as if Serenity has it on speaker phone as well. "After the five minutes were up, the guy opened the trunk, but she won't move." Her voice cracks as if she's terrified for her friend and trying hard to keep it together.

"She won't look at us, won't speak," Serenity continues.

I've heard enough. "Einstein," I say in a tone so flat and low that all four of my brothers snap their heads in my direction. "Get me to her. Now."

A heartbeat later, he's striding through the exit and entering the corn maze as his fingers painted in orange polish fly over his phone screen. I'm right behind him with Boss, Fuse, and Doc following close behind. Boss informs the girls that we're on our way and ends the call.

I may give Einstein shit for being a know-it-all evil genius, but the kid is good. He has us expertly weaving through the maze, never taking a wrong turn or making us backtrack a single time. We pass numerous monsters and masked scarers, but one look at the murderous expression marring all our features has them turning and going in the opposite direction.

In two minutes flat, Einstein rounds one last corner, bringing Serenity and Phoebe into view. They're huddled around an old rusted car with a tall shirtless scarecrow standing off to the side, looking like he's seconds away from pissing his pants. The trunk is popped open, and one glimpse at Addi curled into the fetal position has my steps carrying me straight to the man responsible.

I reach my hands around to the back of my hips and remove the throwing knives I had secured along the waistline of my jeans. I twirl them around and close my fists around the cord-wrapped hilts. Before I can reach the man, Doc rounds my left and Fuse rounds my right, each man putting a hand on my shoulder, stopping me from getting any closer.

"Move!" I snarl out in warning, my rage blinding me to the fact that these are my brothers.

Right now, all I can see are obstacles blocking me from what I truly desire. My fists tighten around my babies in a white-knuckled grasp. They want to taste blood and I'm more than willing to provide them some, straight from the source of a now trembling scarecrow.

"This wasn't his fault," Doc states calmly, nodding his head toward the man I want to hurt.

"If you want to kill him, that's fine." Fuse gains my full attention. "But you'll have to go through us first."

A wicked smile pulls my lips up, and both Doc and Fuse visibly blanche. "Y'all really want to do this?"

"No." Fuse takes a deep breath but holds my gaze. "But like Doc said, this wasn't his fault. He had no idea she'd react that way. Hell, I'm not even sure if Addi knew she'd react that way around a trunk."

The sound of her name acts as an extinguisher to the inferno blazing within me. One second, I'm filled with so much rage I can't think straight, and the next, clarity begins to wash over me like a tidal wave, clearing the bloodlust from my vision. I watch as Boss passes us and approaches the scarecrow.

"I think it's best if you leave now." He speaks calmly, his height causing the scarer to tilt his chin toward the night sky to meet his gaze. The scarecrow nods shakily and disappears through the stalks, not even bothering to use one of the dirt paths. Boss turns and approaches me. "I know you seek retribution. Trust me, we all understand, but you need to put your desires on the back burner because you're the one who has the best chance at bringing Addi out of whatever hell her brain has put her in."

With that, the last of my rage winks out of existence and my shoulders drop. I hate it when he's right. I release a heavy exhale and resheathe my knives behind my back. Both Doc and Fuse release a breath of their own and drop their hands from me, taking a step to the side. I turn to find Einstein over by Serenity and Phoebe, his phone tucked back into his pants as he tries to gain a response from Addi.

I cross the space, the dirt crunching beneath my boots as I come to a stop and tap on Einstein's shoulder. "Here, let me try."

All animosity is gone from my voice as I take in the sight before me. Addi's usual tanned skin is as white as paper. Her makeup is smudged beneath her eyes from crying, and tears stain her cheeks. Her knees are pulled to her chest, her arms wrapped tightly around herself as if she's tried to burrow within her own body to escape the trunk, and tremors wrack her frame. Her chocolate gaze has a thousand-yard stare that breaks my heart into a million pieces.

Einstein moves, and I crouch before the trunk, bringing my face mere inches from hers. I brush a few strands of brown and blonde hair out of her face, tucking them behind her ear. I can feel several pairs of eyes boring into my back, but I couldn't care less if they see me like this. Showing them a side I've never shown anyone but Addi before. A side where all my walls are torn down and laid bare, making me completely vulnerable.

I make sure to keep my voice low and gentle. "Eyes on me, sweetheart."

As if the sound of my voice is the sole cure for breaking her spell, her vision snaps to mine, and a ghost of a smile crosses my lips.

"I feel left out. Here you are, having a party in here, and you didn't think to invite me." I tease and shake my head, feigning disappointment as I brush the back of my fingers over her wet, rounded cheek.

She huffs out a laugh that's weak and shaky, but it's better than nothing. I'll count it as a win. "I—"

She tries to speak, but I stop her with a finger on her lips. "Shh, don't speak, sweetheart. I've got you."

I stand and scoop her into my arms, bridal style. She throws her arms around my neck and buries her head into my shirt. I turn to find everyone gawking at me in a mixture of awe, disbelief, surprise, and gratitude. Without another word, I begin retracing our steps, and everyone falls in line behind me, minus Einstein, who leads the way, his phone back in his hand as his vision shifts between the screen and the path ahead of us.

We're out of the maze just as fast as we entered, and a few minutes later, we're exiting the farm and weaving through the parking lot. Addi doesn't speak, only holds on tight as if she'll be teleported back into that trunk if she lets go. I won't let that happen. Fuse opens the door to my vehicle, and I gently place her into the passenger seat and buckle her in. I had pre-started the truck, allowing the heater time to warm the cabin before we reached it.

I close the door, nod thanks to my brothers, and bid everyone farewell as I climb in and begin to drive us home. Half an hour later, we're pulling into my driveway and parking in the garage. The ride was quiet. Not a strained silence, but a peaceful one that settles around us anytime we're together.

I climb out, round the other side, and carry her into the house. After setting the alarm and slipping us out of our shoes, I carry her up the stairs and straight into her bedroom. After gently placing her down on her bed, I remove some pajamas from a dresser drawer.

"Change. I'll be right back." I place the clothes next to her and leave the room, shutting the door behind me before she can rebuke or utter a single word.

I make quick work of changing my own clothes, putting on pajamas, and heading back to her room. I knock on the door before entering, wanting to make sure she's fully dressed first.

"Come in." Her shaky words flow beneath the crack of the door.

I enter to find her already beneath the covers as I round the bed, strip out of my pajamas, and slide beneath the sheets, lying on my side and facing her with my arm tucked beneath my head.

"Do you want to talk about it?" I tuck a few more stray hairs behind her ear. Her lip quivers as she shakes her head. "Ok." I pull her closer toward me, allowing contact only this once, given her emotional state.

I roll to my back, and she settles against my side, her head resting atop my chest as I stroke her hair in long, slow movements intended to help soothe her. In a matter of minutes, I feel her breathing begin to even out, signaling that she's fallen asleep, and my own lids finally begin to grow heavy.

Chapter 13
SWEENEY

"Honey, I'm home!" I call out in a teasing manner that's become a long-standing joke between us.

I kick off my boots into the hall closet before walking down the hallway and entering the kitchen.

"Hey!" Addi calls over her shoulder as she washes up a few dishes.

I've been away for a week. It might as well have been a damn month as far as I'm concerned. I've grown fond of having her around and seeing her daily. So going an entire seven days without seeing her smile is pure torture. Plus, for the last six months, we've been sleeping in the same bed.

Purely sleeping. Besides harmless flirting every now and then, nothing romantic has happened. Not that I'd be against it if it had, but I know she's still healing. She's come a long way, and I'm so proud of her. I knew she was strong.

Sleeping alone this last week has been… weird, and I don't like it one bit. Looking back, I don't know how I was ever content with being alone. We'd texted all week, but it wasn't the same as seeing and talking to her in person. I was assigned to protect a female celebrity as she attended photoshoots, press conferences, and the premiere of her new movie.

I'd lost count of how many times I caught her making suggestive hints about taking her to bed. If it wasn't already a huge rule of Boss's, it's definitely one of mine. I don't fraternize with clients.

Now, what happens after an assignment is over is a different story. However, even though this woman was gorgeous, she paled in comparison to Addi, and she did nothing for me. Honestly, I found myself comparing her to Addi and found her wanting in numerous ways. Call me whipped, but I couldn't care less. Fuck, Addi and I haven't even so much as kissed each other, and she's ruined me for every other woman on this planet.

I haven't slept with anyone in almost nine months, and Addi moved in only half a year ago. I'd never have sex with someone else if I were sleeping next to her each night, even if we were purely sleeping. It feels… wrong. I told myself I wouldn't do anything until she's ready and makes the first move. I'm proud of myself for sticking to it. The only action I see is from my right hand when I shower. And that's alright because when we do have sex, and I'm confident it will happen eventually, it'll be well worth the wait. I'm a *very* patient man.

I lean back against the island and watch her. She's got her brown and blonde hair pulled into a messy bun, dressed in an oversized T-shirt and a pair of shorts that show just a tease of the crease where her thigh meets her round ass. I allow myself a minute to enjoy the view before I speak again.

The significance of today hasn't eluded me. Though most would consider me a typical male, I at least make it a point not to forget important dates. Especially this one. It's Valentine's Day. Even though I'm single in the eyes of the public, my heart has already been captured. Even if the woman who unknowingly claimed it hasn't acted or voiced it, I belong solely to her.

I'm positive Addi hasn't forgotten what day it is either. Though I'm quite sure she's made it a point to try and forget about this holiday entirely. I don't blame her. If I went through what she did, a holiday built around love would be my least favorite. A constant reminder of the love lost to her, even if Jack never truly loved her. She believed he did, and that's what hurt the most.

I'm confident she's made it a point to stay as busy as possible today so her mind wouldn't linger on what once was. Thankfully, she had work to occupy her time. Now that it's over, it's my turn to help distract her. I tighten my hold on the gift bag I have hidden behind my back. I don't know why I'm nervous. Fuck, I feel like a kid in grade school asking my crush to be my Valentine.

"How was your day?"

She shuts off the faucet and turns to me as she leans back against the sink and dries her hands with a dish towel.

"Busy." She releases a long breath. "Mrs. Sharpe did a second round of interviews for the manager position."

I've learned a bit over these last six months, enough to know that Mrs. Sharpe and her husband are the owners of the bank where Serenity and Addi work.

"How did it go?"

Addi's been busting her ass for months, throwing herself into her work, causing much-needed distraction from her life. In a way, it's given her a goal to solely focus on as she moves up the ladder. She took a huge leap of faith when she applied for the bank manager position, and I couldn't be more fucking proud of how far she's come and all her accomplishments.

"I think it went good?" She sounds unsure but tries to smile through it. "She narrowed the applicant pool down to three of us. I guess that's a good sign if I was called back for another interview."

"I'm sure you'll get the job. You're awesome at what you do."

"I'm glad one of us is confident in my abilities." She snorts before her chocolate eyes narrow. "What are you hiding behind your back?"

I give her a mischievous grin. "Do you want to try and guess?"

"Not at all." She looks apprehensive. "With you, it could be a stuffed teddy bear or a live squirrel you found injured on the side of the road. And everything in between."

She knows me so well. I can't help but chuckle and extend the small purple gift bag toward her. She narrows her vision and takes it cautiously as if it might bite. I wait patiently as she removes the white tissue paper and withdraws the gift.

Her eyes widen, and her beaming smile brightens the room more than sunlight ever could. She grips the coffee mug painted to look like pink marble with the saying *what doesn't kill you disappoints me* etched in shimmery gold.

"I love it!" She throws her arms around me in a hug that's over too quickly before she pulls back to examine the mug again. "Where did you find this?"

I shrug like it was no big deal. "The client I was guarding needed to shop for a few things. I saw it while we were out and remembered you have a weird infatuation with snarky coffee mugs. It screamed Addison."

"Hey, you're the one with a weird infatuation with knives. You're the last person to talk about strange interests." She laughs and I join her as she drops her gaze to the cup and clutches it tightly against her chest. "This one is my new favorite."

Her smile is all the reward I need. "Close your eyes."

She peers at me skeptically. "Why?"

"Just trust me." I laugh. "I'll behave, I promise. Unless you don't want me to." I shoot her a quick wink.

Her narrowed gaze drops down my front and back up again as if sizing me up. Reluctantly, her eyes close.

"You're back in junior high. A boy you've been secretly crushing on finally asks you out."

She laughs but keeps her eyes closed. "What are you doing?"

"Painting you a picture. Duh." I cross my arms over my chest and continue. "He says his parents can take y'all anywhere for a date. Where would you go and what would you do?"

She's quiet for a moment, and I know she's pondering her options. "Hmm, that's a tough one." She bites her bottom lip and tilts her head up, eyes still closed. After a minute, she says, "We'd start with roller skating. Then hit the arcade and finish with some ice cream."

I smile at the vision of her ideal date back when times were simpler. "Alright. Go get dressed."

Her eyes fly open, landing on mine, and her brows pinch together tightly. "For what?"

"For roller skating, the arcade, and ice cream, you silly goose."

Her mouth opens and closes several times, but nothing comes out. I chuckle at her flustered state, but she makes no move to head upstairs to get ready.

"Fine then. I'll go by myself. And fuck, am I going to have fun." I shrug casually and start for the stairs. "Your loss."

I grin when I hear her quiet steps and feel her presence follow me to the second floor. I make it a point not to look back as I enter my room and close the door behind me. I take a quick shower to freshen up before slipping into a pair of blue jeans and a brown and tan flannel button-up. I secure the buttons around my wrists since it's the middle of winter, but I leave the front unbuttoned, exposing the white T-shirt beneath.

After spraying myself with cologne, I leave my room and descend the stairs. I nearly miss a step when I find Addi waiting for me at the front door. My heart skips a beat, and my pulse quickens like a damn teenager when I take in the oversized pastel pink sweater and black leggings that cling to her thick legs and ass magnificently.

Her long brown hair is braided into pigtails, and her makeup looks freshly applied. Her eyes widen slightly as they travel down my front, and her full lips slightly part. The movement makes them shimmer from her gloss, and the sight of the stunning goddess before me goes straight to my groin.

I cross the foyer and slip on my boots. "I take it you finally decided to join me?"

"I'm not one to turn down ice cream." She grins.

"Alright then. Let's go show those kids at the skating rink we still got it in our old age."

"Speak for yourself." She laughs as she follows me into the cold garage. "I'm only twenty-four."

I press the glowing red button on the wall, and the metal garage door begins to open. I round my Toyota Tacoma and open the passenger door for her.

"Yeah, sweetheart. We might as well be dinosaurs to them."

She fully laughs. A sound that has become music to my ears. It makes pride well inside of me to see how far she's come in a matter of months. The night we went to the haunted farm around Halloween, and she had such a bad PTSD attack that it left her physically immobile, was the last time something like that had happened. She's only gotten better from there.

If I had to guess, she's back to being the old Addi again. The Addi I met at that bar. The one so full of life and joy with that can't-stop-me attitude and smartass mouth of hers. The Addi that snared my heart in a trap from just a single look toward her.

<h1>Chapter 14</h1>

ADDISON

Grayson had been gone for a week this time. Luckily, I had work to keep me busy, but those nights were lonely. My nightmares had gone from a nightly occurrence to about once a week. But when he's gone, they're nightly. However, with the help I've been getting from my therapist, I'm now able to wake myself up from them. Not at first, I do suffer a little, but eventually, I'm rousing myself awake.

I knew what today was. I've been dreading the day for a while. Now that it had finally arrived, I forced myself to stay busy at work, so I didn't think about it often. For the last few years, Jack would get me flowers and take me to dinner somewhere fancy. At the time, I appreciated the gesture, but looking back on it, there was nothing special or personal about it. Everyone gifts their significant other flowers and chocolates, and everyone goes out to eat.

I didn't expect Grayson to get me anything or offer to take me out. Why would he? We aren't dating. We aren't even romantically involved. I had planned on spending the evening alone with a bottle of wine or two, popcorn, and a marathon of rom-com movies. But when he surprised me with that beautiful coffee mug, I nearly cried. It was a small gesture, but it was so personal and intimate. He saw something, thought of me, thought I'd like it, and bought it. It's now hands down the most prized and cherished gift I've ever received.

Then he went a step further and had me picture my idea of a perfect date if I were a kid again. It took me a minute to connect with my inner child, but once it hit me, I knew. When I voiced my idea, I expected him to tease me about it. Instead, he's taking me to live that dream. The butterflies I have swarming inside me are an odd sensation I haven't felt in *far* too long.

I can't help but twine my hands together in my lap as I keep my vision trained out the window as he drives us to the skating rink. A foreign sensation hit me when I saw him come down those stairs. The sight of him all dressed up, the way his clothes clung to his broad and muscular frame, had my body waking up in ways I thought forever dead after Jack shattered me into pieces.

Grayson, however, had gathered those pieces into a neat pile, like fallen leaves on the grass. Every full night of sleep I get, every laugh he draws out of me, every time he shapes my lips into a smile, every delicious meal he cooks for me is his way of placing one of those jagged, broken pieces back into their rightful place, like some intricate, master level puzzle that's nearly complete. A task I never thought possible. I'm glad to have been proven wrong. Just this once, though.

The brown of his shirt brought out the beautiful golden hues in his whisky eyes. Then I caught a whiff of his cologne as he walked by. The scent of cedar and fresh rain nearly had me weak in the knees. Now, for some reason, I do feel like a kid on a date with their crush. The nerves, the anticipation, the excitement.

I have to keep reminding myself that Grayson isn't my crush. He isn't someone I'm trying to attract the attention of. He's someone who's become my best friend. Someone who I owe a huge part of my healing to. I can't cross that line with him, even if my body wants to. I'd never risk ruining the wonderful relationship we've built these last six months. Tonight is about letting go and having fun. That's it.

It's no surprise when we pull into the parking lot of the skating rink and find it crowded. It's Valentine's Day, after all. We make our way through the front doors, and suddenly, I'm hit with nostalgia. The small lobby's carpet is black with neon-colored shapes all over it. Old school movie posters hang on the white walls, and muffled music flows through double wooden doors that lead to the main area.

Luckily, we only have to wait in line for about five minutes. I can't help but smile at all the young teens waiting in line with us. Some hold hands with their partners. Others are in large groups of friends. It reminds me of simpler times. When it's our turn, we tell the attendant our skate sizes and Grayson pays.

They buzz us through the door and the full environment envelops me. The rink is packed with people of all ages skating in a counterclockwise rotation, laughter filtering from the concession area, and "Last Friday Night" by Katy Perry playing over the speakers. A projector displays the music video on the far wall of the rink and a disco ball hangs in the middle.

We slip off our shoes and hand them to the workers as they hand us our inline skates. They're black with bright orange laces and a single row of four orange wheels. I'll never understand how people prefer quad skates. I find them too hard to maneuver in.

The same colorful carpet covers the floor here, except for the hardwood of the rink and the tile of the concession area.

We find an empty spot along the row of benches and slip into our skates. After securing the laces, we stand and head toward the rink.

"Have you ever skated before?" I ask as we wait for an opening on the floor.

"I used to play street hockey with the neighborhood kids all the time, but it's been a few years."

A loud bubble of laughter escapes before I clamp my lips shut and pin him with a look. "A few?"

"Keep those smartass comments to yourself," he warns with a smile. Then his eyes shift to mine, finding me studying him. "What?"

"I'm just trying to picture you, all this," I motion with my hands around his large six-foot-three frame, "as a child. I might need to see pictures."

"Don't let my mother hear you say that. She'd have you trapped for hours flipping through old photo albums. I've been this tall since the eighth grade. Thankfully, I filled out muscle-wise shortly after high school. I'm positive I was mistaken for Slenderman a time or two as a teen."

I fully laugh at that as a large group of kids pass and we push off the wall to join the flow of skaters. I lose myself in the music as I skate, Grayson staying by my side the entire time. The songs flow from one to the other, switching between a variety of genres.

I sing along to the ones I know and even catch myself dancing as we make our laps. From the periodic glances toward Grayson, he's doing the same as me. The carefree smile he sports across his handsome face is enough to make any woman's heart stop. I've even noticed a few teenage girls staring. I'm pretty sure he unknowingly set their standards for any future boyfriends, and I don't blame them.

A little while later, the DJ slows the music down so couples can skate together. I go to exit the rink, but warm fingers intertwine with mine, keeping me in the flow of skaters. When I peer down, I find the large hand belongs to Grayson, and an explosion of flutters in my belly has me feeling like a young teenager who is experiencing the effects of attraction for the first time. The feeling is dizzying but in the most addictive way.

"May I have this dance, my lady?" He bows effortlessly as we skate down a straightaway.

I let out an exasperated sigh. "Oh, I suppose."

"Yes!" His free fist is closed as he brings his elbow toward his body in victory.

I can't help but laugh and shake my head. He can be such a child sometimes.

Both brows are raised in surprise when I hear Grayson singing along to "Love Story" by Taylor Swift. "You're a closet Swiftie?"

"There's no closet, sweetheart. I'll scream it from the fucking rooftop if I must." He pins me with a look as we enter a turn.

My stomach drops at that look. I've learned that it can only mean trouble.

"What?"

"I'm going to do it." His grin turns wicked, and he wiggles his thick brows.

"Do what?" My brows are pulled tight in confusion. *What on earth is he talking about?* Then I realize what part of the song we're at, and my eyes widen in fear. "Don't you dare!" He doesn't respond, just keeps that smile that is now causing the butterflies in my stomach to stir in a frenzy. "Grayson, I swear to God, if you embarrass me, I'm leaving."

Right when Taylor sings "he knelt to the ground and pulled out a ring," Grayson pushes past me, pivots so he's now skating backward as we enter the straightaway, and kneels as he sings at the top of his lungs. Though it's been years since he's skated, he's acting as if he never stopped. He holds my hand tight as he belts out the words, and I can feel my face turning beet red with embarrassment.

"Grayson, stand up! People are staring!" I try to pull him up, but it's futile. I try to hide my face in my free hand, but it's no use. "I *will* let you run into that wall!"

Finally, he stands, twists around so he's skating forward again, and throws his head back with laughter. That's it. I'm going to murder him in his sleep tonight.

By the time the song finishes, I'm exhausted and in need of water and a deep hole to hide in. I've lost track of how long we were here. When I glance at the clock, I notice almost an hour and a half has passed.

We return our skates and slip our shoes back on. It takes me a minute to reacclimate to walking instead of skating.

I slap his arm as we exit the building. "I can't believe you did that!"

His tone is full of amusement as we weave through the still-crowded parking lot. "Oh, come on. It was pretty funny."

"You better sleep with one eye open tonight." I point a finger at him in warning as he holds open the passenger door so I can climb into his truck.

He takes us down the road and parks along the street in front of our next stop. It's a combination of a bar and arcade, so we show our IDs as we enter. As I look around, it feels like I stepped back into the 1980s. Arcade games, video games, toys, and decorations from the decade fill the space.

After ordering drinks, we lose ourselves and let our competitive nature shine as we face off and play various games. We played all the classics like Pac-Man, Donkey Kong, Asteroids, and many more. Then we moved on to the life-sized Connect Four and Chessboard. We finished it off with a few rounds of Dance Dance Revolution.

By the time we left and started walking down the street to the ice cream parlor, I was on cloud nine. I hadn't had this much fun in years, and never once with Jack. Not like this. It's effortless when it comes to Grayson. Being with him is as easy as breathing. And I swear, my cheeks and stomach hurt from laughing so hard. I nearly peed myself at least three separate times. One of which was when he tried a dance move on DDR and fell. I had tears from laughing so hard.

"What's your poison?" Grayson asks as we enter the ice cream shop.

I don't care if it's the dead of winter, I can eat this stuff anytime. "Triple chocolate with crushed up Heath bars."

"Good choice." He nods as I relay my order to the worker.

"What about yours?"

"Salted caramel with gummy bears."

I shake my head and accept my order and a spoon. Grayson is handed his next as we sit at a small round table.

"Want to try?" he offers.

"Sure."

He gathers some on his spoon, making sure to get a few mini gummy bears on there, and brings it to my mouth. My eyes widen at the flavor combination I was not expecting. His vision is focused on my lips, and I swear lust flashes through them before he blinks it away.

I clear my throat and gather some of my ice cream on my spoon, holding it out toward him. "Want to try mine?"

He lowers his head and wraps his mouth around my spoon. Heat ignites deep within as he runs his tongue across his lips, and I quickly shift my gaze elsewhere.

"It's good, but it's too much chocolate for me."

"There's no such thing as too much chocolate!" I take another bite of my own before speaking again. "Thank you." His head cocks in confusion, so I clarify. "For this. For tonight. It's been… a while since I've had this much fun."

"I should be thanking you. You put my gaming skills to the test today. I need to practice more."

I smack the back of my hand against his bicep and roll my eyes, but don't stop the smile that seems to shine anytime I'm with him.

Chapter 15
ADDISON

I bolt upright and my hand clutches my chest as I gasp for breath. Fog clouds my brain as I try to recall my surroundings. I peer around the dark space. My bedroom. I'm in my bedroom, not in those woods with the two criminals who were hired to kill me. I release a sigh of relief and swipe my hand across my sweat-slicked brow.

After months of therapy, my nightmares were few and far between, but still liked to torment me. Like the phantom pain of a broken bone that had long since healed, intended to allow you to never fully forget the immense pain you once felt there. This nightmare had gone further than ever before. I've long since mastered being able to rouse myself out of them, but T had finished his assault on me, and Baldy was undoing his pants before I finally regained control and forced it to stop.

That never happened. Thankfully, they never got the chance to hurt me, aside from a few punches to the face, because Grayson showed up and killed them both before they got the chance. I release another breath of relief as my breathing returns to normal and I peer down to find Grayson sleeping peacefully beside me. He's on his back with one arm bent and tucked beneath his pillow, the angle making his bicep bulge deliciously. The covers have fallen to his waist, fully exposing his strong, muscular chest and impeccable abs that I've considered running my fingers along far too many times to admit.

His face is slightly turned away from me, giving me a stunning view of his chiseled profile. The steady rise and fall of his chest confirms that I hadn't roused him with my nightmare. I twist and tap the screen of my phone to check the time. It's a little after midnight. I quietly release a third exhale and gently rise from the bed, tiptoe across the carpet, and ease the door open. After slipping out of the room, I close the door behind me and enter my bathroom.

The bright light causes my eyes to squint until they reacclimate. I hiss at the cold as I splash water over my face and pat it dry. After brushing my bed hair out and securing it in a messy bun, I turn off the light and exit the bathroom. As I pad down the hallway toward the stairs, I can't stop my eyes from darting toward the reading nook now veiled in shadows. I have yet to catch even a glimpse of Sharleen, which has me wondering if Grayson made up the old lady spirit just to fuck with me.

If so, I'm already working up a plan that will put his to shame. Payback can be a bitch. I descend the stairs and take a seat on the couch. I'm wide awake, and instead of lying in bed until I eventually grow tired again, if I do at all, I'd rather watch a movie I've seen a million times in hopes that sleep overtakes me soon. We'd both been so worn out from our Valentine's not-a-date that after we got home and showered, we went straight to bed and fell asleep within minutes.

A smile tugs at my lips at the reminder of last night. Skating, arcade games, and ice cream, it truly was one of the most perfect nights of my entire life. I grab the remote and turn on the movie *The Goonies*. That always does the trick. I've seen it dozens of times and I'm usually nodding off before Chunk can do the truffle shuffle.

"Can't sleep?" a deep voice sounds from behind me, and I nearly jump off the couch in fright.

I let out a startled scream and clutch my hand to my chest again, my heart racing for the second time in a matter of minutes. Which I'm sure isn't healthy for the precious organ.

"Didn't mean to spook you." Grayson laughs, rounds the couch, and sits on the opposite end.

His pajama pants hang low on his hips, teasing the muscular V that disappears beneath the waistline. Either he couldn't find his shirt in the dark, or he didn't bother with it before coming to find me, because his torso is completely bare, and I find it hard to peel my eyes away. Finally, I manage as I shift my gaze back to the TV.

"It's alright." I force myself to take a few slow breaths, willing my heart rate to even out again. "I'm sorry if I woke you. I tried to be quiet when I slipped out."

"That didn't wake me up." He gives me a reassuring smile.

I turn and arch a brow toward him. "Did you have a bad dream?"

He shakes his head. "No."

"Then what woke you?"

"The absence of your presence." His confession steals the very breath from my lungs. "I guess sleeping next to you for months has trained my body to notice when you're not there." He laughs it off as if it's nothing, but I can't ignore the warmth that spreads through my chest. No matter how hard I try. "What woke you?"

A small half-laugh slips out. "I'll give you three guesses, but you'll only need one."

"Do you want to talk about it?" His voice is gentle as he shifts so he's facing me and stretches his long legs toward me.

I do the same, careful so our legs don't touch.

"Not really." I release a heavy breath.

It doesn't go unnoticed how his honey vision trails down the expanse of my bare legs exposed by my pajama shorts. I swear I catch heat momentarily flaring within them before he blinks and his gaze returns to normal, shifting back up to my face. Great… Now my precious organ is racing for a completely different reason.

"Alright." He nods and tilts his chin toward the ceiling as if pondering something. "Have you lived in Oklahoma your whole life?"

The sudden subject change is a bit jarring, but a part of me is thankful. I truly didn't want to talk about my dream, but I didn't want to sit here in silence either.

"Yep, my father has worked for ONG since before I was born and retired a few years ago. They still live in the same house they bought right after getting married."

A grin pulls at one side of my mouth like it always does anytime I think of my parents. I envy their connection. I will never take for granted their healthy relationship that showed me what marriage is supposed to be like with your partner. A relationship I thought I'd found with Jack. How utterly wrong I was.

"What about you?"

"Nah, my dad was in the Army my whole life. We never stayed in one place longer than three or four years."

"That must've been hard." Sympathy fills my tone.

I couldn't imagine moving that much in one's lifetime. I knew the kids I graduated with since pre-K. All one hundred and thirty-four of them. Growing up in a small town has its perks, and also, its disadvantages. I've never done much traveling, aside from a handful of family vacations each year.

"Not really." He shrugs and smiles. "I've always been quick to make new friends, and I got to see more of the world in my youth than most see in their lifetimes. My family's always been close with each other, so we did alright."

I don't miss the way his whisky eyes fill with love when he talks about his family, and I love that he had that amazing support growing up. Not everyone is that lucky.

"You're a handful now." I laugh. "I can only imagine what preadolescent Grayson was like."

A full smile spreads across my face at the thought of him as an ornery child.

"I definitely kept my parents on their toes." His laugh is full, and the sound lightens my heart. "The principals had my parents on speed dial with how often I got into trouble from pulling pranks on people, both students and staff."

"Somehow, I'm not surprised." I laugh and can't help but tease. "I don't think you've changed much after entering adulthood."

"I haven't." He shakes his head. "But don't tell my parents that. To them, I'm a mature, well-respected adult now."

I burst out laughing at that, wrapping my arms around my middle. My stomach hurts and water lines my eyes by the time I calm down.

"Hey, I'm not that bad!" He slaps my leg playfully and shakes his head incredulously. "I doubt you were much better. What was your childhood like?"

"I was an angel," I defend myself. It's his turn to snort, and I slap his leg in return. "Though I'm an only child, I never felt alone. My parents were and still are the best. I still am a total daddy's girl." A bright smile pulls my face up at all the wonderful memories I shared with my father, and Grayson mirrors it with one of his own. "He never missed a practice or a sports game. He taught me about cars and allowed me to help him restore an old 1960s Chevy truck, which was a passion project of his. Instead of spending my weekends with friends at the mall, I sat on the couch with him watching SportsCenter, following our favorite teams: football, baseball, basketball, hockey. You name it, we watched it."

"Your dad seems like a good man." He chuckles.

"The best." I release a happy sigh. "Never once had I seen him angry, but after my parents learned about what happened with Jack, I saw a side of my father I'd never seen before. There aren't words to express how furious he was with the man."

The memory of that day flashes through my mind. The day I visited them and had to tell them the ugly truth and everything that transpired back in Hawaii. My face was mostly healed from the split lip and bruising, but you could tell I had gone through something bad. My mother held me while I cried my eyes out for what felt like the millionth time, and my father sat there at the kitchen table with a look of murderous rage swimming through his eyes.

"I know." His words have my brows furrowing in confusion. "He reached out to me and asked me to meet him for a beer."

My jaw drops at this new piece of information and my brain swirls in confusion. My father never mentioned to me that he'd ever met Grayson before, let alone had a beer with him.

"What? When? How?" I can't get myself to formulate sentences longer than a single word.

He crosses his arms over his chest and shrugs innocently. "I don't know how he got my number, but I received a phone call the day after you visited them. I agreed and met him later that afternoon."

I sit up straighter and pull my knees in close to my chest, giving Grayson my full attention. "What did he want?"

"He wanted to know what happened and told me not to spare a single detail. So, I did." He shrugs again, like it was no big deal to meet with my father and discuss things behind my back. I'm not upset, just flabbergasted. "I'm guessing he wanted to make sure the man his daughter was staying with was not another Jack. Or worse. I'm guessing I passed his test because he thanked me and shook my hand before we departed."

I had no clue. It's been half a year since then. How has neither Grayson nor my father ever mentioned that they know each other? My heart swells with love for my father for wanting to check in on me and vet my new roommate.

"Holy shit…" I mumble the curse and shake my head slightly in disbelief.

He fully laughs at my flustered state, the sound filtering around the otherwise quiet room.

"Addison Thatcher is at a loss for words. I need to write this down in the history books."

"Fuck off." I roll my eyes, but can't stop myself from joining him in laughter.

Time ceases to exist as we lose ourselves in conversation about the most random crap, and before I know it, my eyes grow heavy. I don't remember drifting off to sleep. The last thing I can recall is Grayson telling me a story about the senior prank he orchestrated back in high school. Then I feel myself being lifted into a pair of strong arms, and the smell of cedar and fresh rain assaults my nose as I bury my face in the wonderful warmth that surrounds me.

Our elevation changes and I can only assume we're climbing the stairs. Then, I feel myself being laid against something soft as the wonderful warmth retreats and is replaced by something lesser. I toss and turn, searching for that previous warmth, and begin to settle when I find it again. I remember getting as close to it as possible before a deep sleep overtakes me and I'm back on that beach in Hawaii, with my toes buried in the sand and Grayson standing next to me, our fingers interlocked. The dream stays like that until morning comes.

Chapter 16
SWEENEY

It's been a week since our unofficial date on Valentine's Day. Never in my entire dating history have I had as much fun with someone as I did with Addi. As I continue to do each day that I'm with her. I look forward to coming home knowing that she'll be there. And maybe I shouldn't get so comfortable, so attached, but that would be like telling the sun not to rise. Inevitable.

I find Addi on the couch, cuddled under a blanket with a book in her hands.

"Why aren't you reading upstairs?" I lean an arm atop the couch and peer down at her.

"And risk seeing Sharleen? Or accidentally sit on her? No, thanks." She bookmarks her page and sets down her book.

I chuckle, knowing Sharleen isn't real. I just made up the story of a harmless old lady's spirit haunting the house to pull her leg, but I'm not about to tell her that. I'll make her sweat over it a little bit longer.

"Congratulations." I can hear the smile in my own voice.

She peers up at me in confusion but giggles. "What are we congratulating?"

I can barely contain my excitement. "You kicking ass and getting that manager's position at the bank."

Pride fills my tone at how far she's come. She still sees her therapist, but they've cut back on the frequency of appointments to every two weeks. She's genuinely smiling and laughing again. She's back into her old smartass ways, and even though I want to fuck the brat out of her, I'm grateful. I can't tell you how long it's been since she's had a bad day.

She's been actively searching for her own place for a while now, but I keep finding reasons why they're bad choices. Some of my points are legit, I promise. I'm not about to let her move into any old place, especially if I know it's in an unsafe area. Others I pull out of my ass so she can stay living here. I'm not ready to let her go, and if I'm picking up on her feelings correctly, which I'm positive I am, she isn't ready to leave just yet either.

I remove the hand that I have hiding behind my back, and her chocolate eyes widen at the bouquet I'm gripping. It's a pop of tropical-colored roses, mums, and solidagos, accented with beautiful green foliage. Yep, I'm putty in her hands. I'd do this every day if I got to see that pure happiness on her perfect face.

"Grayson, they're beautiful!"

She gasps and takes the flowers, bringing them to her nose and taking a long inhale. I've never wished to be a flower a day in my life, but at this moment, I'm jealous of them. The sound of my name on those lips of hers goes straight to my dick, and I have to allow myself a few deep breaths before I speak. I know if I don't, she'll be able to hear the lust that lingers there.

"Go get dressed."

"For what?"

"I'm taking you out to celebrate." I give her a wink before striding out of the room to get ready myself, not giving her the chance to refuse.

Thirty minutes later, I'm downstairs, leaning against the kitchen counter as I wait. I fidget with the cuffs of my navy-blue button-up dress shirt that I have tucked into a pair of form-fitting black slacks. The sound of heels clacking against the hardwood floors draws my vision to the hallway. When Addi comes into view, I swear my heart stops beating.

She's got her hair tied up into a tight bun with a few curly brown strands framing her round face, fully exposing the column of her slender neck. Her long-sleeve plum sweater clings to her torso in the most delectable way, and her ankle-length black skirt has a slit running up her right leg that stops mid-thigh. Her four-inch, black-heeled boots peek out beneath her skirt, stopping just below her knees. A goddess indeed.

After having my fill of drinking her in, my gaze finds hers roaming over me. *Take your time, sweetheart. It's all yours.* When her eyes finally meet mine, a sexy blush creeps across her cheeks that I know doesn't belong to her makeup.

"I wasn't sure how dressy I should go, but I feel more confident in my choice after seeing you," she says a bit breathily and nervously.

I can't help the drop in my tone. Not when I'm looking at the vision standing before me. "You look fucking stunning."

Her blush deepens and I feel triumphant. "You look fucking stunning yourself."

"I know." I shoot her a cocky wink, gaining an eye roll from her.

I've got a mental tally of just how many times over the last six months she's given me a reason to fuck the brat out of her. So far, we're at fifty-three. I motion with my hand for her to start walking toward the garage, and I relish every second I get to admire that plump ass of hers in that tight skirt. My hands twitch at my sides, and I clench my fists to resist the urge to grab handfuls of the supple flesh.

I open the passenger door of my truck and extend a hand to help her in. "My lady." I bow playfully.

"My lord." She curtsies back before placing her hand in mine and climbing in.

I don't miss the euphoric sensation that occurs when our hands connect. And by the slight hitch of her breath, neither does she. There's still ice and snow on the roads from the winter storm we got the other day, causing me to switch to four-wheel drive so we don't risk sliding or getting stuck anywhere.

Twenty minutes later, we're entering the city and pulling into a concrete parking garage. We get out and make our way down the street toward the restaurant. The slight chill in the air has her looping her arm through mine as she walks close to my side, trying to stay warm. We enter the building, and I smile at her sigh as the warmth of the restaurant hits us.

"Good evening," a young woman greets us with a smile. "Do you have a reservation?"

I feel Addi tense next to me, but I speak before she does. "Yes. Two, under Grayson Rider."

"Perfect! Right this way." She grabs two menus, and we follow close behind as she takes us to a table near the back. "Enjoy your meal." She departs with a smile.

"How did you get a reservation in such a short time? This place always has a waitlist," Addi inquires as she sits and picks up her menu.

"It does." I shrug casually. "That's why I made the reservation earlier this week."

Her chocolate eyes snap up to mine as they widen. "But I didn't know I got the promotion until this morning."

I give her a satisfying grin. "I was confident you'd get the job."

"Well, that makes one of us," she mutters as she resumes looking over her menu.

We order and lose ourselves in conversation. Talking with her is as easy as breathing. There's never any awkward silence, and we never run out of things to talk about. An hour and a half and a bottle of wine later, we're making our way back to the parking garage. Addi's a giggling mess beside me as she clings tighter to my side now that night has fallen, and the sun has taken what little warmth it offered.

A feeling I could get used to. Ah, who am I kidding? I got used to the feeling of her at my side or hanging on to my arm as we walked a long time ago. I know I shouldn't have, but like I've said before, I'm confident she'll be mine one day. Whether it's months or years from now makes no difference as long as the end result is Addi living under my roof as something more than just my roommate.

As we enter the dimly lit parking garage, I get an uneasy feeling in my gut. If years of working in my profession have taught me anything, it's to listen to those feelings. My vision slides across the garage, trying to pinpoint the danger.

Addi's in the middle of telling me something that happened at work the other day when a tall, slender man veiled in black steps out between two vehicles about ten feet in front of us. I halt my steps and position myself between her and the stranger. She gasps in fear and her grip on my bicep tightens.

"Give me your wallets!" the man shouts.

His breath clouds before him from the cold, and he's got a pocket knife gripped tightly in his gloved fist. His arm is extended, pointing the sharp steel blade towards us. I arch a brow at him before throwing my head back and roaring with laughter. I feel Addi tense further behind me, but I keep my gaze trained on the mugger.

"Why the hell are you laughing? Didn't you hear me? I said give me your fucking wallets!" If the thug's face wasn't covered in a black ski mask, I'd bet money it's red. And not because of the cold.

"Oh, I heard you." I laugh some more before speaking again. "A knife, man? Really?" My vision drops to the pathetic excuse of a blade. "If you can even call it that. Please tell me that's not your only weapon."

"No! I've got a gun behind my back. And if you don't give me your fucking wallets now, I'll shoot the little bitch!"

Liar. If he had a gun, he'd be using it to mug us instead of the knife. What he called Addi now has me wanting to paint the walls with his blood. It would brighten up the otherwise boring grey concrete of the parking garage. But I remain calm and keep a carefree grin across my face, which only serves to rile the criminal up further.

"You know lying is a sin. Right?"

"Fuck you! I'll say it one more time before I cut up the whore's pretty little face." The man turns his vision toward Addi.

I hold out my hands, showing him that I'm unarmed as I slowly bend and reach down toward my right shoe. I act as if that's where I keep my wallet. The criminal tenses and shifts his feet into a fighting stance, preparing to attack if I make any sudden movements. I keep my movements slow and deliberate as I pull up the hem of my slacks and remove a large, sleek black throwing knife I keep secured within my sock.

"Mine's bigger." I smile wickedly at him as I stand and flip the blade through the air, catching the tip between my finger and thumb. The feeling of a possible fight always gets my adrenaline pumping, and fuck, if I don't love a good fight. "Want to see who's faster?"

After a few heartbeats, the mugger pivots on his heel and takes off running. With the flick of my wrist, I send the blade flying. It sinks deep into the man's right calf, causing him to cry out in pain as he falls to the concrete floor.

"Stay here," I instruct Addi as I take long strides and catch up with the criminal in a matter of seconds. "Did you think I'd let you go just so you could mug another unsuspecting couple?"

"Fuck you!" he shouts as he removes my knife from his flesh and throws it to the ground. The metal clatters against the concrete floor, painting it red with his blood.

"I've got more if you'd like to see them. One even curves at the tip, making it great for carving." I smile at him, causing his eyes to widen in fear as he shakes his head. "Drop your knife." He does. "Is that your only one?"

"Y-yes."

My smile widens at his second lie, and I begin to unbutton the cuff on my right arm, pretending like I'm going for another hidden knife.

"Alright! Alright! Fuck!" he shouts and tosses a second pocket knife to the ground.

"See, honesty truly is better." I chuckle as I bend down to pick up my throwing knife. He flinches as I draw closer to him. "Uh, you can have that back." I begin swiping the blade clean of his blood against his black pants. "Now get the hell out of here before I change my mind on letting you live another day of your pathetic life."

Without hesitation, the man jumps to his feet and runs away, half limping from the wound in his calf. I collect my blades and his. I retuck mine into my sock and toss his in a nearby trash can before making my way back to Addi, who's still standing right where I left her. She's got a look of shock marring her rounded and slightly pale face. She's shivering, and I don't know if it's due to the cold or what just happened, but I make quick work of getting her into the truck and blasting the heat.

After a few minutes, I ask, "Are you ok?"

"Ask me that once we're home." Her teeth are still chattering as she holds her palms in front of the now-warm vents.

Home. The word hits me like a freight train, and damn, I'd be lying if I said I didn't like the sound of that. Scratch that, I fucking love the sound of that. I don't even try to stop the smile that touches my eyes as I drive us home.

Chapter 17

ADDISON

I don't think I fully relaxed until after we got back to the house, and I defrosted in a hot shower. I had an amazing time at dinner and that mugger had to go and ruin it. I was frightened at first, but when I remembered who I was with, I knew things would be ok. And if I'm being honest, watching Grayson handle that criminal the way he did, so effortlessly, was kind of hot. I may have been a little turned on, but I'll take that secret with me to my grave.

However, I nearly jumped out and offered to walk back, cold be damned, after what I let slip. It's not that I didn't mean it, or that I regret saying it. His house does feel like my home, but I didn't mean for him to hear that little confession. Now I lie in bed next to him, silence filling the air between us as I search for something to say. For the first time, I feel nervous in his presence, and I don't know why.

"Do you always stash knives in your socks?"

He turns on his side to face me, tucking his hand beneath his head atop the pillow. "You don't?"

"No." I laugh. "Actually, I don't think I know a single person, aside from you, who does."

Though, after how he rescued me in the woods in Hawaii and how he handled that criminal tonight, his call sign couldn't be more fitting.

"Huh." His gaze shifts toward the ceiling as if lost in thought.

I begin picking nervously at invisible lint on the sheets. "Thank you."

"For what?" Two creases form between his thick brows as his golden eyes meet mine.

"For earlier, with the mugger."

"Eh, just another Tuesday." He waves it off with his hand. "I'll accept payment in the form of a kiss anywhere of your choosing." He jokes and rolls to his back, interlocking his fingers behind his head.

I don't know what comes over me, but I do just that. Without thinking, I extend across the bed and place a quick peck against his warm, smooth cheek. I quickly fall back to my place on the mattress and bring the covers up around me, as if hiding behind them will shield me from him. God, I feel like I'm a ten-year-old girl who just kissed her first crush instead of a grown-ass woman who's experienced with men.

His head snaps to the side as he pins me with a heated look. "What was that for?"

His voice is so low that it sends my toes curling into the sheets and butterflies fluttering in my stomach. Or maybe that's my nerves. Who knows?

"Payment, as you said." I keep my voice light and send a silent thank you that my words didn't come out shaky. "Good night."

I flip over, putting my back to him. He's still for a moment before I feel the mattress dip around me. His presence consumes me, the scent of cedar and fresh rain assaulting my senses. He comes closer and places a gentle kiss on the back of my head.

"Good night, sweetheart," he whispers in my ear, and his breath against my sensitive skin sends a delicious shiver through me.

His presence retreats as he settles into his side of the bed. *Holy shit… What are you doing, Addison?* I scold myself for crossing a fine line we drew months ago. This is only going to complicate our relationship, possibly strain and/or ruin it. I can't do something like that again. Unfortunately, my body doesn't get the memo, and my mind keeps replaying that kiss and his last words as I drift off to sleep.

"Because every time I was with her, I pictured it was you!" Jack's voice rises another octave. As if noticing it, he takes a deep breath and releases it slowly.

The confession hits us like a bird flying into a windshield. Hard and ugly.

"What the fuck!" I shout now that I've had some time for the shock to wear off. I'm beyond pissed.

Jack turns to me and speaks calmly. "Didn't you ever wonder why I never said your name during sex or usually buried my face in the crook of your neck?"

"I thought it was weird at first, but I just figured it was one of your quirks."

"It's because if I said a name while coming, it would have been Renny's name on my lips, not yours, and there was no getting around trying to explain that one. Anytime I entered you, fucked you, came inside of you, I pictured it was her I was doing all those things to. You were just a hole to use."

"You fucking bastard!" I storm toward him and slap him. He allows the first one but catches my wrist when I go to swing a second time. "Did a part of you ever love me?" My voice breaks as tears fall in rivers down my cheeks and realization hits me about the sickening truth of the man I'd chosen as my life partner. "Was there any part of this that was real?"

"No," he says to me coldly. "I think we're done here. Gentleman," Jack calls to the two men still sitting on the couch, "she's all yours. You know what to do."

Before Baldy can throw me over his shoulder, the living room, everyone around me, the entire world begins to blur and fade away. I find myself standing on a beach, my toes digging into the warm sand, and Grayson standing at my side. Our fingers are interlaced as we peer out toward the horizon together.

We don't speak. We never do when my nightmares fade away and are replaced by this. We always stand there, side by side, in complete and comfortable silence as we gaze out over the water together. Peace as I've never known settles over me, and I know I'd be content to stay right here for eternity.

My eyes crack open, and I peer over at the alarm clock. The red illuminated numbers inform me it's just after eight in the morning. I allow my heavy lids to close again as I release a sigh, wishing for only five more minutes. Maybe ten? Fifteen. Fifteen more minutes, then I'll get up.

I focus on the warmth that surrounds me, and I slowly wiggle backward, trying to push myself further into it. In this cold winter, I welcome the entirety of that addicting heat.

"Addison," a gravelly voice sounds from behind me. Every muscle in my body freezes. My eyes fly open wide, and I don't dare breathe. "Wiggle like that against me again, and I won't be held accountable for what'll happen next."

Oh God… My mind is racing as I force the sleep from my brain. Fully aware of my surroundings now, I can feel Grayson behind me. Feel every part of his front that touches every part of my back. My eyes drop down to see a strong arm draped around my middle. I take a breath and push my ass a millimeter further back. *Holy…* I feel every inch of his hardened member that's pressing against the crevice of my ass.

My mouth goes dry, and I twist my head, peering behind me. He's got his face buried in my hair, the tip of his nose brushes the back of my neck, and every nerve in my body is sent into hyperdrive. I swallow hard, and my breath quickens as butterflies begin to wake me up more than coffee ever could, and a foreign ache pulses deep within my center.

"Why…" I keep my vision trained on the wall across from me and take a deep breath to steady my voice before trying again. "Why are you spooning me?"

"Because you had another bad dream."

A breath later, I feel his body tense behind me as if he realizes what he just let slip and didn't mean to voice it. I believe my lungs refuse to function properly.

My question is a whisper. "Excuse me?"

"I… Fuck…" I hear him curse under his breath. I turn in his hold to find his whisky gaze trained on mine.

"Is this… Do you do this often?" My vision shifts between his eyes.

He lets out a long breath before answering. "Yes. I leave for work before you wake up, so I'm not surprised you don't know."

I open my mouth to speak, but close it, unsure of what exactly to say to that. "I swear, on my sister's life, I don't ever touch you. Not like that. I never have. I only hold you against me. It…" Pain and fear flash through his vision as if he knows he's crossed a line.

"It what?" My words are clipped.

"It helps you relax. Your nightmares wake me up, so I pull you against me, and it settles you."

Holy shit… No. It can't be.

My voice sounds miles away. "And you do this *every time* I have a bad dream?"

"Yes." His eyes frantically search my face as if what I'm thinking would be written across it.

Oh, God… That means…

"Addi, please—"

I don't give him the chance to finish his sentence. I can't. I need space and air, both of which I can't find if I stay in this bed, in this house with him.

"I… I've got… a yoga class with Renny in half an hour. I have to go."

I slide out of his hold before he can stop me and bolt from the room. I fly down the stairs, not even bothering to grab my shoes as I take my keys in hand and leave the house. I can hear him shout my name, hear the desperation in his voice, but I shut the front door before he can reach and stop me. I don't even notice the icy cold sidewalk beneath my bare feet as I jump into my Challenger, fire it up, pull out of his driveway, and take off down the road.

Chapter 18
ADDISON

"So, you just ran?" Serenity asks as she hands me a steaming cup of coffee.

I didn't realize where I was driving until I pulled into Hunter's driveway. I nearly sent the poor man into a panicked frenzy when he answered the door in nothing but a pair of pajama pants hanging low on his hips, his long brown hair spilling down over his shoulders. Luckily, it's Saturday morning, and they're both home. By the looks of it, he'd just woken up too. He took one look at me, standing in my pajama shorts and an oversized T-shirt with no shoes in the dead of winter, quickly ushered me inside, hollered for Serenity, and asked where Sweeney was and if he was hurt.

I quickly reassured him that Grayson was ok and that I needed to talk to my best friend. Serenity rushed down the stairs wearing nothing but Hunter's missing T-shirt, took one look at me, and led me by the hand into the kitchen. Without her asking a question, I started unloading what happened as she made us coffee with a bit of liquor mixed in. I didn't care that it wasn't even nine in the morning yet.

"Yes, like a fucking coward." I take a sip of the coffee and relish the burn and warmth the liquor causes within my chest.

"Oh, honey, you aren't a coward," she reassures me as she takes a sip from her cup.

But I am. Instead of explaining myself to Grayson, I ran. Just like the night I first asked him to sleep in the bed with me to test a crazy theory I had. How was I supposed to tell him the truth? How was I supposed to tell him that every time I had a nightmare, at varying spots, it faded away and turned into the same dream? Me and him standing on the beach, holding hands. That every time I had those bad dreams, it was him pulling me into his hold that caused my nightmares to shift into dreams of tranquility.

"I am because if I told him the truth, it would change everything." My voice cracks and I take another sip. "And I'm afraid of that change. He's been so valuable to my healing. What if I lose him as a friend because the feelings aren't reciprocated?"

"Addi," Serenity sighs as she places her hand gently over mine. "After what you went through with Jack, it's understandable that you would have reservations about entering another relationship. You're not going to lose him. Give him the benefit of the doubt. He's a big boy and one that deserves the truth."

I let out a long breath. "I know."

Hunter finally enters the kitchen and heads straight for the coffee pot. He's pulled his long brown hair into a knot on the back of his head, and much to my dismay, has found another shirt to cover himself with.

"For future reference, you don't ever have to cover your body in my presence." I toss at him teasingly, even though my mood isn't as playful as usual.

He throws his head back in laughter and Serenity smiles brightly.

"I'll keep that in mind for the future." He pours himself a cup, spies the bottle of Kahlua, and arches a brow towards us.

"Girl talk, honey."

"Ah." He nods in understanding and takes a sip of his coffee. "If you tell me Sweeney did something to deserve this, I can make sure to put him on the most sufferable assignments for the next few months as punishment."

I can't help but chuckle. "No, he did nothing wrong."

"Explains why he called me in a frantic state, asking if I'd seen you."

I cringe, knowing I caused Grayson unnecessary worry. "What did you say?"

"I told him you were here safe and that you'd go back when you were ready. He didn't like that, but he's a big boy." He gives me a reassuring smile.

I drop my vision to my half-empty mug, zoning out on the way the liquid swirls around the cup.

"I don't know the full story, but I've always been pretty good at reading my surroundings. A little bit of advice? Just talk to him. Trust me, it won't go the way you're fearing."

Hunter walks over, places a soft kiss atop my head, and shoots Serenity a wink before leaving us alone again.

"If you let him go, I'll snatch him up."

Serenity joins me in laughter and follows Hunter's retreating form with love filling her green eyes. "I don't plan on it."

I allow myself a deep breath before I push open the front door and step inside, shaking off the cold. I climb the stairs and head straight for the bathroom. Since I left in such a rush this morning, I freshen up before descending the stairs and pad down the hallway. My heart doubles in pace when I find Grayson sitting on a barstool at the island. His elbows are propped atop the counter, and his chin rests atop his closed fists. The moment I'm in sight, his vision snaps to me, but he doesn't move.

"Hey." I sigh as I walk to the other side of the island and lean my back against the counter, facing him.

He doesn't speak. He sits there quietly, waiting for me to explain my earlier actions.

I drop my gaze to the floor and begin to pick at the hem of my shirt. "I'm sorry… about bolting like that. I… I panicked."

I peer up at him to find his brows furrowed, with concern filling his honey gaze. Still, he remains quiet.

So, I take a deep inhale. He deserves the truth whether he likes it or not. Whether his feelings are the same or not. I'm a grown woman and can handle rejection if that's what it comes down to. I have plenty of money for my own place if this goes badly and I have to move out. Shit, I still have over three million dollars of Jack's money that I split with Serenity stashed away in accounts that I refuse to touch. I'll be alright.

"You've been so significant in my healing journey that I'll never be able to thank you enough. You make me laugh when I want to cry. You hold me when I do need to cry. You've coaxed me out of so many panic attacks. You've made sure I started eating and sleeping properly again." I clear the emotions from my throat before continuing.

"My nightmares used to be a nightly occurrence. After our… arrangement… I started noticing that anytime I had a nightmare, at varying spots, it would begin to fade away and turn into a dream. A peaceful dream. Always the same one."

I hold his whisky gaze, and the intensity I find staring back at me has my stomach flipping. He hasn't so much as moved a muscle. If it wasn't for the occasional blinking, he'd pass for a statue.

"Do you remember that day at the resort? The next day after… After everything with Jack. I was standing barefoot on the beach, looking out over the water." He nods once. "You came up to my side, took my hand in yours, and stood there with me. I was so lost in grief, drowning in my pain, that I couldn't see my future. I couldn't remember what happiness felt like. I wanted nothing more than to walk out into that water and keep walking until the tide pulled me out and washed all the pain away."

My voice cracks and I clear the emotions from it a second time. Grayson's face is masked, but worry and sorrow dim the brightness of his beautiful gaze as if he remembers that day like it was yesterday.

"You didn't say a single thing. It was as if you knew I didn't need words, but simply that I needed not to be alone. That I needed to be reminded that I'm *never* alone, and I made it out. You were my anchor to reality. You kept me from drifting away in that water. You stood there with me for what felt like hours."

A bubble of laughter rolls up my throat as I quickly wipe a few tears from my cheeks with the back of my hand.

"Well, anytime I had a nightmare, and you'd pull me against you, somehow, I knew I was in your arms. My subconscious knew I was safe because the bad would fade away, and the next thing I knew, I'd be standing on that beach hand in hand with you by my side. My dream would stay like that until I woke. But I always woke up alone, so I never connected the dots. I thought it was my mind returning to a peaceful time, but it was my body telling me where I belonged. With you… in your arms."

I clear my throat for a third time, wipe away a few more fallen tears, and breathe deeply before meeting Grayson's gaze again. He's still sitting with his chin resting atop his closed fists, his eyes studying me intently.

It took some time and numerous sessions with my therapist to realize that what I had with Jack, the love I thought I had with him, was something I had fabricated in my head. I had this picture in my mind of a beautiful future, a handsome man, a white picket fence, kids running around with a combination of both our features, us living a comfortable lifestyle because of his amazing job. But that future I had built up, the perfect box I tried to fit him into, had blinded me to the truth of the man I thought he was. The man I wanted him to be.

He wasn't some perfect specimen. He wasn't head over heels in love with me. I wasn't marrying the other half of my soul. He was never mean or abusive toward me, but his affections were fictitious. My therapist helped me break down the entirety of mine and Jack's relationship, helping me to finally see the truth. I had blinded myself to all the red flags that should've raised concern over time because I wanted that future I had designed so badly that I had settled for the first man I thought could provide it to me.

After living with Grayson for half a year, and even though we aren't dating, I've seen exactly how a real man is supposed to treat a woman. And the fact that I'm merely his roommate and he still treats me like a queen only proves how lesser of a man Jack truly was. I wish I could've had this awakening before I walked down that aisle. I wish I could've avoided all the pain and heartache Jack caused both Serenity and I. But we can't change our pasts. We can only learn from them and grow from our mistakes, shaping us to be a better version of ourselves each time.

I know with every fiber of my being that what I did with Jack is not what I'm doing with Grayson. I don't know if it's because he's grown to be one of my best friends without romantic feelings blinding us to reality, but I see the honest depths of his soul. I know I'm not fabricating some dream with him. What I see, his kindness, his loyalty, his devotion to the ones he holds dear, his love, it isn't make-believe or warped because I'm trying to fit him into some perfect box. It's real. *He's* real.

"Anyway." I begin picking at my shirt hem again. "That's why I bolted. I… I got scared. Scared of a possible relationship with another man. Scared of possibly being hurt again. Jack had shattered me to a point I feared was beyond repair, but you proved me wrong and helped heal me. I don't think I would survive being broken again. I was also scared of the truth. That I'm…" I take one more deep breath. "That I'm falling for you, Grayson."

A few heartbeats pass, each one feeling like minutes, before he pushes off the counter, rounds the island, and comes to a stop in front of me. I hold my breath as I peer up at him, his large frame blocking out most of the room. Still, without speaking, he cups my face in his large, calloused hands. His touch is gentle but firm as he forces my gaze up to meet his.

"I'm not Jack. I would never push you into anything you're not comfortable with, and I'd never hurt you as he did. I swear it on my life."

My vision shifts between his, seeing the complete honesty behind every word he speaks. I know he's nothing like Jack. He couldn't be further from that spawn of Satan. It's just my fears and PTSD trying to take over and control me, trying to sabotage my future. Jack had completely shattered my trust in men, in ever possibly dating again. But Grayson, he's used love to help heal me. So much so that I can see a possible future with him. One more wonderful than I ever could've imagined and that scares me even more.

Then he lowers his head and captures my lips with his. There's nothing soft or gentle about it. His tongue demands entry right away, so I tilt my chin up and open for him, my arms coming up to wrap around his neck. It's hot, fast, and filled with hunger and need.

This man doesn't just kiss with his mouth, but rather uses his entire body to convey his feelings. Grayson kisses with a purpose, with such passion that it has the ability to make me forget my name if I'm not careful. He eliminates the remaining space between us, and my soft curves melt against his hard, muscular frame. He tastes like power and coffee, and my toes curl with desire.

I feel one of his hands drop from my face as the tips of his fingers trail a path down my back, leaving goosebumps in their wake, before it lands on my ass. He spreads his large hand and squeezes firmly, drawing a moan from me that vibrates against our mouths. He groans in response before he pulls back. We're both breathing heavily as he rests his forehead against mine.

"I've been yours since the day we met. I've just been waiting for you to realize it and for you to be ready. It's about fucking time, sweetheart."

Chapter 19
SWEENEY

With my forehead still resting against Addi's, I slip the tips of my fingers into the waistband of her pajama shorts, slide them over her round ass, and let them pool around her ankles. This woman seriously bolted out of the house in these thin clothes, in the dead of winter, barefoot. The thought is enough to have me teasing her until she screams in frustration as punishment.

Later, though. I've waited over six long months to taste her, to have her. I've spent every night in this house lying in bed next to her, dreaming of the day I finally get to claim her. That was a kind of torture I'd never wish on my worst enemy. To see the pure beauty of her skin, follow the softness of her curves with my gaze, and smell her intoxicating strawberry aroma, but unable to take it further. Pure. Fucking. Agony.

I don't think I can go slow and savor her properly if my life depended on it. And by the way her body is responding to mine, she's craving my touch just as badly. Later. I'll take my time later. Right now, the need to be inside of her is stronger than the earth depending on the sun for warmth.

I pull my head back and love the way her eyes are closed with a look of pure lust softening her rounded features. Those lips of hers are slightly parted as she waits patiently for me to make my next move. My vision shifts lower to take in the way her baby-blue panties hug her ass, leaving just a bit of flesh showing. *Such a fucking tease.* The sight is enough to drop grown men to their knees.

Like her shorts, I slide them down and let them pool at her feet before making quick work of gripping her hips and hoisting her atop the counter. She gasps at the sudden movement and the sting of the cold counter against her bare ass. Her chocolate gaze locks on mine and pure desire swirls within, further driving me wild.

I don't need a mirror to know a pure predatory and satisfactory look contorts my rugged features. The way those thick thighs of hers squeeze together is proof that she likes what she sees. With a hand on each knee, I spread her wide and drop before her.

She follows every movement as her chest rises and falls with quick, short breaths. I shoot her a wink before peering straight ahead to her freshly shaven sex that's now glistening and bared for me, ready to be feasted upon. After going almost a year without tasting a woman, I'm famished.

"Scoot toward me." My voice is low as I dig my fingers into the supple flesh of her thighs, holding her legs open wide. She does, and I waste no time in running my tongue up her center in a long, slow drag. "Fuck, sweetheart. I knew you'd taste amazing."

She gasps at the sensation, and her hand goes straight to my hair, running her fingers through the short brown strands and holding tight. Her grip sends a slight sting that goes straight to my hardening erection, causing it to twitch painfully against my pants.

Her other hand grips the edge of the counter in a white-knuckled grasp.

I allow myself one more slow pass before the last of my restraint snaps, and I devour her. I taste every inch of her pussy, inside and out, as I fuck her with my tongue.

"Grayson!" she moans. The sound is better than any melody, sending me into a frenzy like a shark when it scents blood.

Her grip on my hair tightens as I insert a finger and clamp around her clit, biting down before swirling my tongue to ease the sting. By the sounds emanating from her, she's loving every bit of it. As am I. I insert another finger and relish in her tight warmth. The way her soft walls grip me, I know will be the death of me when I finally fill her with my cock.

"Oh, shit!" She rests her head against the upper cabinets. "Don't you dare stop."

I wouldn't dare stop, not when I'm starving to drink her in. I hook my fingers and begin hitting that spot that I know will send her over the edge. In confirmation, I feel her clench around me, and she screams in pure ecstasy as her orgasm floods her body.

I don't stop my feast until I watch her body relax atop the counter and she's left panting. I allow myself a few more measured passes with my tongue, making sure I clean every bit of her finish up. I was right about two things. She's absolutely delicious and a screamer.

I hold the two fingers I had inside her in front of her mouth. "Want to taste how delectable you are?"

She nods eagerly as she begins to suck them clean. The feeling of her tongue swirling around them has me envisioning it's my dick she's doing that too, and I nearly come in my pants like a damn teenager. Yeah, I need to get her upstairs. Now.

I step between her legs and wrap them around my waist. Her arms suddenly wrap around my neck as I remove her from the counter and start walking toward the stairs.

"Where are we going?"

I love how weak and shaky her words are, knowing I'm the cause of her flustered and half-sated state.

"The first time I fuck you will not be atop a counter, Addison."

I flash her a wicked smile when I feel her legs tighten around me from my words. I take the stairs two at a time and stride down the hallway toward her bedroom. A bedroom I've been sleeping in for the last six months. I toss her atop the bed and notice her gaze shifts to my shirt. I peer down to see a wet spot where her sex rested against the fabric.

"Look at that." I tsk. "You made a mess, sweetheart." Lust drips from my words as I pull my shirt over my head and discard it somewhere to the left.

"Maybe you should've cleaned me up better." She sucks her bottom lip into her mouth, and my cock flexes in response.

"My apologies." I place my hand over my bare chest. "I'll be sure to correct that mistake next time." I observe the way her toes curl into the comforter at my sinful promise. "Remove your shirt."

She sits up, grips the hem of her T-shirt, and lifts it over her head so agonizingly slow. Inch by inch, her stomach is bared to me, then a sexy ass belly button ring, then the bottoms of her breasts, then her collarbone, before the fabric is fully removed and tossed aside. My gaze travels over her as I try to memorize every square inch of her supple body. A woman's body. So full and soft and…

"Fucking perfect." I shake my head in full satisfaction.

She slips her lip between her teeth again as her gaze drops to my pants. "Your turn."

I'm only happy to oblige. I slip my pants and boxers down my legs and don't miss the way her eyes widen as my fully erect cock springs free.

"Yeah, that's all yours, sweetheart. Yours to taste, to play with, yours to enjoy."

"All mine?" she whispers sheepishly.

I step out of my clothes and climb onto the bed. "Since the day we met."

Addi lies back and parts her legs as I hover over her, one hand on each side of her face, and peer down at her. I take a mental picture of the sight before me. Her, lying beneath me, fully naked with a slight flush painting her neck and chest. Her brown and blonde strands sprawled atop the comforter. She looks like a goddess, and I want to spend hours, days, weeks even, simply worshiping her body.

Her gaze snaps to mine and her face contorts in question. "You… You haven't been with anyone since I moved in?"

"Since a few months before we met, if I'm being truthful. You've ruined me for every other woman on this planet."

She places her hands over my wrists and slowly runs them up, over my muscles, around my shoulders, and down the divots of my abs. I groan in pleasure and flex at the sensation. God, I've dreamed about this for so long. What the softness of her palms would feel like against my heated flesh. It's better than I ever could've imagined and is nearly enough to bring me to completion.

"Have you been with anyone since?" I cock my head to the side.

A blush creeps across her cheeks as she meets my gaze. "Only Bob."

My body tenses and my fists dig into the covers. A mixture of emotions has my jaw flexing. Hurt, anger, jealousy. I thought she wasn't ready to be with anyone while she recovered. When did she sleep with Bob? *How* did she meet him? *When* did she meet him? Did she sleep with him during the times I was out of town?

I try hard to get a grip on my emotions. She's a free woman, not mine. Not yet, at least. She's free to be with whoever she wants to. But damn if she didn't just rip my heart out.

I take a calming breath. "Who the fuck is Bob?"

"Battery-Operated Boyfriend." She blushes further. "My vibrator."

She can't stop the full smile that brightens up her beautiful face. Then she laughs. She fucking laughs. Clearly finding much enjoyment in my agony.

I release a sigh and feel my muscles relax again. "That damn vibrator," I mutter and shake my head.

"Jealous?"

She holds my gaze, amusement dancing through her eyes as she wraps her hand around my throbbing erection. I buck at the sudden sensation and groan in pleasure as her grip tightens.

"Very."

I grit out the single word through clenched teeth as she slowly begins to stroke me. So slow that it's fucking torture and pure pleasure at the same time. She brushes her thumb over my swollen head, and I moan. I need to be inside of her. Now.

I begin to lower my hips as she aligns my erection to her slickened entrance, running the sensitive head up and down her opening, teasing us both in the process. Her eyes flutter close, and she moans softly. Though this is pure torture, I hold my position, allowing her to use me for her pleasure. I let her remain in control. If she wants this, wants me, then she'll direct me inside of her. If she isn't ready or changes her mind, she'll stop me.

But please, for the love of all things holy, let her fucking want this, want me as much as I think she does. As if in answer to my silent plea, she meets my gaze, pure desire looking up at me.

"Grayson," she whispers as she tugs on my shaft again.

I understand, and with a single thrust, I bury myself in her heated center. "Fucking hell, sweetheart!"

I groan as I still, partly to give her body time to adjust to my size but also because she's so damn tight that I would've come within seconds if I kept moving. It's been a while. She gasps, and I feel her hand grip my shoulders as her nails dig into my flesh.

I groan again at the pain and the pleasure it shoots straight to my dick. She could treat me as a scratching post, could draw blood, and I'd relish every sting. Soon enough, her hands cup my ass as she tries to pull me further into her.

I arch a brow and give her a playful grin. "Do you wish for me to start fucking you now?"

"Yes," she practically whines.

I drop my head and begin placing a trail of kisses from the base of her neck, up, over her jawline, and stop at her ear. "Then beg for it, sweetheart."

"Grayson, please." She wastes no time. "I *need* you to move." Pure desperation fills her voice. A desperation that mirrors my own.

Satisfied, I withdraw to the tip and plunge back in, over and over in slow, deliberate movements, wanting her to feel every inch of me. The way my cock fills her with each plunge will be my undoing, I'm sure of it. Though my hands are itching to cup her ass so I can angle her hips, allowing me to drive deeper inside of her, I keep my hands planted beside her head and my torso tilted up. I can't take my eyes off her. I love the way her eyes fill with pure lust, the way her mouth parts in ecstasy, the way her tits bounce with each connection of our hips.

"Shit! Just like that!" She arches her back, pushing her full breasts further into the air. "Yes!"

I quicken my pace and pound into her harder, rougher. Call me an addict, because one taste of her sweet pussy now has a death grip over me. I know I'll never be able to get enough. I'll never tire of the feeling of moving inside of her. It's like her body was meant just for me, as if her tight heat was molded to house me.

I slide a hand around her throat and squeeze. Not enough to cause harm, but enough to hold her firmly in place. The sight of her lying beneath me nearly has me spilling inside of her, but I refrain. I'm not ready for this to be over just yet. Her chocolate vision slides up to meet mine, and complete trust fills them. Trust and desire.

"Tell me you're mine."

I peer through the windows to her soul. A soul that called to me that first day like a lighthouse to a ship. A soul that mirrors my own. A soul that, when put together with mine, makes a perfect whole.

"I'm yours, Grayson," she pants with a lazy smile. "I'm all yours." Those words have my movements growing erratic. Then she repeats my words back to me. "Tell me you're mine."

I give her a wicked smile. "All." I thrust once, hard. "Fucking." Another hard thrust. "Yours." Thrust.

Her eyes flutter close, and I pick up my pace, knowing we're both so close. After a few more thrusts, Addi explodes around me. She screams my name as her walls constrict tightly around my dick, bringing my finish to the surface.

"Addison!" I groan as I spill deep inside of her, marking her and finally claiming her as mine. I don't stop until I've emptied myself and we're both left panting as we come down from the highs of pleasure.

Reluctantly, I withdraw and immediately miss her warmth. I plop down on the bed and pull her to my side. She props herself on her elbows and peers down at me as I gently run my fingers through her silky brown and blonde strands.

A single tear cascades down her cheek, and I swipe it away with my thumb. "Was it that bad?" I tease, keeping my voice light despite the fear trying to creep in.

Does she regret what we did? Did she not enjoy it like I did? Did she misinterpret her feelings for me? My mind is racing with a hundred possibilities, and my heart is thudding painfully against my ribcage.

"No." She sniffles and gives me a shaky smile. "You… You looked at me."

Out of all the fears I had, that was never even in the realm of possibilities. Why wouldn't I look at her? She's perfect.

I cock my head to the side, and my hand stills halfway through her strands. "I'm not sure I understand."

She takes a deep breath, and a ping of hurt crosses her features before she pushes it away. "Jack…" She takes another deep breath and swallows audibly. "He always used to keep his face buried in my neck anytime we… And he *never* said my name. He… He confessed that I was only a hole for him to use. That anytime he was inside of me, he pictured he was doing that stuff to Renny, and if he said a name, it would've been hers."

Her voice cracks and another tear slips free. I swipe it away and my heart shatters, but rage also tries to consume me. Who the hell would ever do something like that, let alone voice it aloud? Jack was truly a piece of shit, and his death was too easy. It should've been drawn out over days, weeks even, of intense torture until he begged and pleaded for death.

"The only woman I'm thinking about is you. The only name I want to scream is yours," I cup her cheek and hold her gaze, showing her the God's honest truth behind every word. "I never want to stop watching you, sweetheart. You occupy my every thought. You're the very air I breathe. You're my sole reason for existing. It's you and only you. Has been since day fucking one, sweetheart."

A soft sob escapes from her, but she quickly recovers and crashes her mouth against mine. Our tongues instantly tangle as I close my fist around her silken strands, holding her there until we nearly suffocate. When she pulls back, we're both breathing heavily with a fresh wave of hunger filling our gazes.

"I can't believe that just happened." She sighs contentedly and begins to trace idle circles across my chest with her fingers.

Her simple touch and the slight ticklish feeling of her fingertips brushing against my heated skin are enough to have fresh blood rushing to my dick.

"About damn time," I tease.

She slaps my chest, but I see a bright smile lighting her face. Knowing that she's naked, lying in my arms, and full of my finish has me ready to go again.

"Would this be a bad time to tell you I found a new place for myself?"

I still beside her as my lungs refuse to work and my stomach drops. "I beg your pardon, sweetheart?" I speak in a very slow and dangerously low tone.

Still propped on her elbows, she sucks her bottom lip between her teeth and peers down at me. "I… I found an apartment close to work. It's in a wonderful neighborhood, and they said I could move in today if I wanted to."

I can't tell if she's joking or not right now. After what we just did. After she told me she was mine and I said the same to her, how does she still want to move out? Did it mean nothing to her?

"So help me God, Addison." My words are clipped. "You better be joking."

She fully sucks her lips between her teeth and bites down to fight the smile trying to surface. Then, she bursts out laughing and… That's it. This woman will be the death of me. With that smartass mouth of hers, she's going to give me either an aneurysm or a heart attack.

In a matter of seconds, I hover over her back, grip the back of her neck, and push the side of her face into the covers. She gasps in surprise but doesn't fight me.

"Someone likes to play games," I whisper in her ear before sucking on the sensitive lobe. She lets out a breathy moan that has my body flooding with delicious anticipation. "I love games, and I'm *very* competitive." I dip my hips so my freshly hardened erection presses into the crease of her bare, round ass. Her eyelids close lazily, and she moans again. "And you know what, sweetheart?"

"What?" she pants.

I remove my hand from the back of her neck and grip a fistful of her hair. I tug backward, gaining a hiss from her that turns into a moan as I force her back to arch further. Her eyes peer over her shoulder at me, waiting for my response.

"I always win." My smile is devilish. "Now, push that round ass of yours up for me."

She bites back another moan and asks, "Why?"

Like she doesn't already know why. She wants to hear me say it, and I'm more than happy to oblige.

"So I can fuck that smartass attitude of yours back into submission."

I grind my erection into her ass again. Pre-cum already beads at the tip with excitement. I know I just had her, but it wasn't enough. It won't ever be enough. Like an obedient girl, she pushes her ass into the air, and I drink in the sight before me.

Her bare body is fully exposed. Her back is arched to me in a way that makes her round ass more inviting. A mixture of our finishes began to leak out of her entrance and smear across the top of her thick thighs.

"Good girl," I growl in her ear as I rub my swollen head through the mixture, using it as lubrication, and align myself with her entrance before thrusting inside of her again.

Chapter 20

ADDISON

"You slept with Sweeney?" Serenity gasps, her mossy eyes as wide as saucers.

The sound echoes off her office walls, and I'm thankful that it's lunchtime and the bank isn't too busy. Since she got promoted to loan officer and gained her own office almost two years ago, we've had lunch here together nearly every day.

"Why don't you shout it a little louder? I don't think the tellers working the drive-through heard you." I shake my head and instantly feel a blush warming my cheeks.

"Sorry," she whispers with a grimace. "But holy shit!" She's trying hard to contain her excitement, and all I can do is laugh. "Was it good?"

"The things that man can do with his tongue and his…" I clear my throat, feeling my blush deepen. "Should be illegal."

"Oh, my." Serenity starts fanning herself with a napkin. "I need details, girl. Start from the beginning."

"Well, after our talk, I went back home and told Grayson the truth. One thing led to another, and we spent the entire weekend in bed. So much so that I'm pleasantly sore and will be for the next few days."

"Home?" Serenity perches a brow high on her head.

I pause and the realization hits me. Then I smile. "I can't begin to explain it, but yeah. Home."

"I'm so happy for you! For both of you! I knew Sweeney had a thing for you since that day at the bar."

I roll my eyes at my best friend, at my chosen sister. The feeling of seeing her, of seeing ourselves in our old ways again, makes my heart feel whole. After the events following my wedding, I thought we'd never be able to get back to this type of normalcy. I'll forever be thankful for Hunter and everything he did to help Serenity through her trauma and get back to her true self once more. Just as Grayson did for me. As he continues to do each and every day.

My first week as manager of MoneyFirst Bank is almost at a close. I was nervous about applying for the position, but after throwing myself into work these last six months, craving something that would keep my body and mind busy, I've slowly been climbing the ladder. Then I was told I got the job, and I knew all that hard work was worth it.

The entire staff has been nothing but supportive and happy for me and my accomplishments. Well, all except Paul Nelson. He also applied for the manager's position. However, he did congratulate me, and after this week, I feel there are no hard feelings between us.

It's Friday, which means my and Serenity's weekly dinner date with delicious mixed drinks. However, this week will be our first time adding two more people to this tradition. We've invited our boyfriends for a double date. Though it's weird to refer to Grayson as my boyfriend.

What do you call someone who's your best friend and lover? A title that doesn't make us sound like teenagers. I'll have to think about it, but things are official between us after we slept together last Saturday and voiced that we belonged to each other. The memory sends butterflies soaring across my belly, and I can't help but smile. The thought of such a powerful, dangerous, and sexy man like Grayson belonging to me alone is empowering in such a way I never knew existed.

"Are you sure you don't want me to wait with you?" Serenity turns off her computer and gathers her belongings from a drawer of her desk.

"No, it's ok. I just have a few more things to finish up, and then I'll be out of here. Go ahead and snag us a table before they're all taken by the dinner rush. I'll meet y'all at the restaurant." I shoot her a wink.

Honestly, I shouldn't be more than twenty or so minutes behind them. I just have to finish closing up the bank for the night.

"True." She laughs and slings her purse over her shoulder. "Is Sweeney meeting us there?"

"Yep. He sent me a text a few minutes ago saying he was about to head that way. Hunter?" I follow her out through the empty lobby toward the doors.

"Same." She digs her car keys from her purse. "Well, don't stay too long. Do what's necessary. The rest can wait till Monday. We've got margaritas to drink." She shoots me a wink before leaving.

She was the last employee to leave, so I make quick work of finishing up my tasks and closing up the bank for the night. Half an hour later, I'm returning to my office to retrieve my belongings.

My phone buzzes in the pocket of my slacks, causing me to pause at the doorway to my office. I remove it, lean against the doorframe, and smile when I see a photo of a smiling Serenity, Hunter, and Grayson resting in our group chat.

Serenity: Cheers! HURRY UP GIRL!!

Grayson: Hurry up! Or I'll eat the entire appetizer myself.

Addison: I thought I was your appetizer?

Grayson: You're a fucking full-course meal, sweetheart!

Hunter: Gross. This isn't a private chat. You know that, right?

Grayson: Don't listen to him. He's just jealous because you took me from him.

Hunter: Again, gross.

Serenity: I'd watch you two together. (tongue-out emoji)

Addison: Same! (raised hand emoji)

Grayson: What do you ladies think happens when we're on an assignment together? Those nights away from y'all get very lonely…

Hunter: How do I leave a group chat?

I shake my head, and my laughter echoes through the quiet bank. A beaming smile works its way across my face as I begin typing out a response, but before I can finish, something heavy slams into the back of my head, and the world around me goes dark.

My head is pounding when I open my eyes, as if a member of a rock band is performing an intense drum solo inside my skull, only to immediately shut them again due to a blinding light. I groan at the pain, and my other senses begin to slowly return. Grayson's sweet voice calling my name draws my eyes open again.

He sounds frantic. Why? Did something happen? Why does my head hurt so much? I feel like I'm going to throw up. I blink away the blurriness of my vision to see Grayson hovering over me. His large hands cup my cheeks as he gazes intently into my eyes. Serenity is kneeling on my other side with a look of panic and worry across her angular features.

Hunter is pacing back and forth across my office as he holds his phone to his ear. I haven't the slightest clue who he'd be talking to.

"Addi, can you hear me?" Grayson's words are more audible to me now as I shift my gaze to him.

My voice is weak as I ask, "Why are you here?"

"Thank fuck." He blows out a breath as he grips my hand and slowly helps me into a sitting position.

I hiss at the pain throbbing through my head and reach around to rub against it. "What happened?"

"That's what we're trying to figure out," Serenity says calmly.

Hunter hangs up his phone and squats down on his hunches at my feet. "The cops are on their way. How are you feeling? Does anything hurt?"

"My head," I groan as the room tries to spin.

"How many fingers am I holding up?" Hunter moves his hand.

I squint, trying to focus better, but it's futile. "Uh… two?"

"Are you nauseous?" Hunter inquires further.

I take a slow, deep breath through my nose. "Very."

"You're most likely concussed." Grayson stays calm, but there's a hint of strain evident in his tone as he rubs small circles across my back. The feeling helps tremendously in putting me more at ease. "The paramedics can confirm when they get here."

"Will someone please tell me what the hell's going on?"

"You never showed up at the restaurant, Addi." Serenity's voice is filled with worry. "We tried texting and calling you, but you wouldn't answer."

"Einstein tracked your phone and said you were still at the bank." Grayson's whisky eyes are frantic as I peer up at him, listening intently. "So, we rushed here, Serenity used her badge to get us in, and I found you lying unconscious in your office."

"What's the last thing you remember?" Hunter questions.

"Uh…" I pause, trying to recall my last memory. Though it hurts too much. "I was about to leave when I got y'all's group texts. Then everything went black."

Hunter lets out a long breath before glancing around my office. "No one touches anything. The bank should've been locked up for the night if you were about to leave, but the vault was wide open when we got here."

"You think someone robbed it?" Serenity's voice pitches with growing fear.

"It's possible. Would explain why Addi was knocked out." Hunter's brows furrow, and I swear I could see the gears turning in his mind. "Sounds like they may not have wanted witnesses."

Movement next to me draws my attention to see Serenity remove her cell phone. Her fingers fly over the screen before she pulls it to her ear.

"Mrs. Sharpe, it's Serenity Jinx." She pauses, and even though it's quiet in the space, the immense pounding in my skull doesn't allow me to hear the other end of the conversation. "Yes, ma'am. I know it's late, but it's an emergency. You need to get down to the bank. I believe there's been a robbery."

Mrs. Sharpe responds and then Serenity hangs up the phone.

"Trash can," is all I'm able to get out as I clench my jaw and desperately try to hold my lunch inside.

Grayson doesn't hesitate and has a small black trash can in front of me a few seconds later. Serenity and Hunter exit the room as I throw up while Grayson holds my hair and rubs circles across my back. When I'm confident I won't puke again, he helps me to my feet. I sway a little, but his firm grip on my hips keeps me from falling.

The cops, first responders, and Mrs. Sharpe show up a few minutes later. Before anyone has the chance to question me, Grayson escorts me to the ambulance to get checked out. Besides a confirmed concussion, I'm in good health.

After questioning Serenity, Hunter, and Grayson, the cops finally ask for my story. I wish I had more to tell them, a description or something, but I thought I was truly alone in that bank. I didn't even see the hit coming. Finally, after what felt like hours, Grayson took me home, helped me shower, and held me until I fell asleep in his arms.

Chapter 21
ADDISON

I don't know what I did to deserve such bad luck these last six months, but maybe I should cleanse myself. I don't remember breaking a mirror, or a black cat crossing my path, or walking beneath a ladder, or spilling salt without taking a pinch and tossing it over my left shoulder. However, bad luck seems to be attracted to me like a moth to a flame.

First off, everything that happened the day after my wedding to Jack. How he was only with me to get close to Serenity. How he took out a multi-million dollar life insurance policy on me and then hired two criminals to kill me so he could live the rest of his life with Serenity. It sounds like something straight from the pages of a thriller novel, and it was a nightmare I never thought I'd wake up from.

Then I had to go and have a horrible PTSD episode a month later while we were out celebrating the Halloween season. It was my first time going out in a social setting after the incident, and all I wanted to do was let loose, get scared out of my pants by monsters and masked strangers, drink some beer, and eat some good food. But no.

My trauma had to pick that night to throw me into one of the worst panic attacks I've ever experienced after I was tossed into the trunk of a car while in the haunted corn maze. My body locked up so badly, and my brain took me far away from my friends, back to Hawaii, as I was forced to relive the horrors that occurred on that island. I felt as if that was what hitting rock bottom felt like. Thankfully, Grayson got to me and was able to pull me out of the dark pit my mind had locked me away in.

Months passed and I thought things were starting to look up. Therapy has been a major help. I couldn't tell you the last time I had a bad day, my nightmares are a rare occurrence, and I'm truly smiling again. Then, while out to dinner with Grayson to celebrate the promotion I got at work, some idiot thought it was a good idea to try to mug us. Not with a gun, no, with a damn pocketknife of all things. Honestly, it was a bit offensive. Thankfully, knives are Grayson's thing. Weird, but whatever. I wasn't complaining, though, when he handled the criminal and sent the guy running like a coward.

You'd think it would stop there, right? Hell no. When it rains, it fucking pours. During my first week as a bank manager, someone had to knock me out and rob the place. I wish I were joking, but this string of bad luck has become my unfortunate reality. Who did I piss off to end up cursed like this? I wish someone would tell me so I could make them the biggest cake ever and pour my heart out in an apology in hopes they'd lift the curse.

The only good thing that's happened to me lately is Grayson, and I will never take that for granted. It's been two days since the robbery, and finally, the headache from my concussion is gone. I should've been back at work this morning to start a new work week, but the bank is still closed while the authorities investigate the crime.

I haven't the slightest clue how that's going, what was taken, or how much. I haven't heard a peep from the cops since I gave them my statement the night of the incident. Which is weird because, since I'm the bank manager, you'd think they'd keep me in the loop with the investigation. Maybe they decided to leave me out since I was there when it happened. Even though I didn't do anything. Ugh, who knows? My only hope is that whoever did this will be caught soon and all the money and valuables recovered.

I nearly had to shove Grayson out of the house this morning. He didn't want to leave, not with what just happened, but he has a security job that's taking him out of town until tomorrow afternoon. I promised him I'd be fine. I told him that my plans consisted of the flatscreen in the living room and his secret hidden snack stash. He laughed but I could read the worry etched into his stupidly beautiful face.

Not worry about his snacks, but rather about leaving me alone. However, I did just that. I found his hidden stash the other week when I was putting away some groceries in the pantry. I had to pull a chair over and stand atop it to reach the top shelf so I could move some things around and unpack the new food. Stashed in the back corner was a plastic sack that contained sticks of beef jerky, a bag of caramel popcorn, a can of salt and vinegar Pringles, as well as candies like Nerds, Sweetarts, and sour gummy worms.

I swear, I'm dating and living with a child. He'd hidden it well too, using his height to his advantage. Though I'm tall for a woman, standing at five-foot-eight, I'd never known it was there if I hadn't been standing on a chair. I'd munched on it while I binged

Jersey Shore. I didn't dare watch any of the trashy dating shows he's grown fond of. He'd consider it cheating and probably kill me.

That night, I lay in bed and snuggled his pillow, breathing in the scent of cedar and fresh rain that lingered on the fabric. No matter how hard I willed sleep to take me, it never came. So, I opened my dresser drawer, pulled out my vibrator, and sent a picture to Grayson of me playing with myself. I wish I could've been a fly on the wall when he received the photo so I could watch his reaction.

Instead, he sent me a photo of himself in the shower with his hand gripping his hard cock. Touché. I ended up pleasuring myself to the thought of him jerking himself off, and after my orgasm, sleep finally took me. I did have a nightmare about running through those woods with the two hired thugs after me, but I was able to easily wake myself up.

The next morning, I woke to the sound of my phone ringing. I groan as I blindly feel for it where it rests atop my nightstand. I unplug the charger and answer it.

"Hello?" I try to clear the sleep from my voice.

A male voice I don't recognize responds. "Hello. Is this Ms. Thatcher?"

I'm instantly wide awake and sitting up straight, fearing the worst. That this is a call letting me know something happened to Grayson. My heart skips a beat and my stomach churns with unease.

"Yes." The word is shaky.

"This is Detective Anderson. I'm one of the officers looking into the robbery at MoneyFirst Bank."

"Oh." I blow out a long breath. "What can I do for you, detective?"

"We have a few questions pertaining to the incident we'd like to ask you. Are you free to come down to the station today?"

"Yes, of course." A bad feeling begins to take root in the pit of my stomach, making my question come out hesitant. "Am I a suspect?"

"We just have a few questions we would like cleared up is all."

The detective keeps his tone calm and respectful, but doesn't answer my question, which puts me further on edge.

"Okay. I'll be there in about an hour."

After hanging up, I quickly dress in a pair of blue jeans and an oversized grey sweater before throwing my hair up into a bun, putting on a light layer of makeup, and I'm out the door.

Luckily, the rest of the ice and snow had finally melted from the winter storm we'd gotten. My Challenger has all-wheel drive, but I hate driving in the snow. An hour later, I walked through the front doors to the police station and told a female uniformed officer working the front desk that I had gotten a phone call from Detective Anderson, who had questions about a case he was working on. The woman directed me through the metal detector and buzzed me into the back of the station. I followed her down a few hallways and past an open room filled with rows of desks and officers at work.

She opens the door to an interrogation room and instructs me to have a seat, and that the detective will be in shortly. The carpeted room is small, only large enough to fit a rectangular metal table and three chairs. Nothing adorns the walls except for a single clock and a large rectangular pane of glass. I've seen enough cop shows to know that it's a two-way mirror and that I'm most likely being watched from the other side.

I thought my nerves were bad this morning, but now? They're all over the place. I'm thankful I didn't have any breakfast. I'd probably be seeing it again in a less appealing manner right about now. I pull out a chair and take a seat. About twenty minutes later, two detectives enter the room.

"Hello, Addison. I'm Detective Anderson. I spoke with you on the phone this morning."

Anderson is a tall, middle-aged Black man with a shaved head and a caterpillar of a mustache that's rather impressive.

"This is my partner, Detective Gomez."

Gomez is shorter, middle-aged as well, with dark bronzed skin, short black hair, dark chocolate eyes, and a five o'clock shadow darkening his upper lip.

"Hello." I nod nervously.

"Do you prefer Addison or Addi?" Gomez inquires as he and his partner sit in the two chairs across from me.

"Addi is fine."

Anderson sets a manila folder atop the table, and my eyes dart to it, wondering what's in there. *Is it hot in here? Why am I so nervous? I'm the victim. I did nothing wrong.* I repeat that last statement a few more times as I coach myself through a few deep breaths.

Anderson speaks with what appears to be genuine concern filling his voice. "How are you feeling, Addi? Does your head still hurt from the concussion?"

I fiddle with my hands in my lap beneath the table. "It's better now, thank you."

"How long have you worked for MoneyFirst Bank?" Gomez inquires.

"A little over four years now."

Anderson fires off the next question. "How long have you been the bank manager?"

"A week." Two creases form between my brows. "I'm sorry, am I in some kind of trouble?"

"We just wanted to ask you a few questions," Gomez responds.

"It feels like an interrogation."

Anderson arches a thick brow. "Do you have something to hide?"

"No. Do you?" I challenge and cross my arms over my chest.

Gomez chuckles and responds with, "I've got a secret or two I'd like to stay buried in the closet."

I snort in response. "Be straight with me. What's this about?" I'm tired of the twenty-question game already.

"Do you know what was stolen from the bank?" Anderson inquires.

I raise a brow at the men and cock my head to the side. "Do y'all do this on purpose?"

Both men spare each other a glance before shifting their vision back to me. "Do what?" Gomez scrunches his face in confusion.

"Take turns speaking or asking questions like that. First, you speak." I point to Anderson. "Then you." I shift my finger to Gomez. "Anderson, Gomez, Anderson, Gomez." My finger continues to shift between them.

They both chuckle, but as I suspect, Anderson talks next. "We've been partners for over a decade. Sometimes you accidentally fall into a routine that ends up working for you." He shrugs a shoulder. "Back to my question. Do you know what was stolen from the bank?"

"No." I sigh. "After the paramedics looked me over, an officer took my statement, and I was free to go home. I haven't been contacted or informed about anything that's going on. For all I know, the thieves could've already been caught, but since I'm here, I'm guessing that's not the case."

I immediately shift my gaze to Gomez, who I know will speak next. He picks up on it and chuckles lightly to himself. "You said thieves as in multiple. How do you know it wasn't a solo job?"

"Because when I closed up that night, the vault was shut. After I came to, my friend told me the vault was open. It takes two people to open it. So, there must've been at least two thieves."

My eyes shift to Anderson. I wonder if they're being predictable on purpose to try and distract me or throw me off, see if I slip up somehow.

"Your friend?" Anderson asks and opens the folder. "Hunter Gatlin?" I nod. "How would he know the door was open? Could he have been a part of it?"

"Hunter?" I can't help the bubble of laughter that escapes. "Hell no! Neither he nor any of the men who work with him could ever do something like this. They're good guys. And he's ex-military. He's been trained to take in his surroundings and observe every little detail. It's actually kind of scary sometimes."

Both detectives laugh as if they know from experience the kind of men I'm talking about.

"How do we know you didn't have help?" Gomez inquires.

"Uh, because I was knocked out?" My tone sounds like I would've said *duh, isn't it obvious?*

"Your partner could have crossed you. Knocked you out after y'all bagged the money?" Anderson suggests with a casual shrug.

My stomach churns further and I feel the color drain from my face. "You don't think… I… I didn't do this."

"The owner, Mrs. Sharpe, said the same thing. She vouched for you, saying you wouldn't hurt a fly and that you were one of her best employees," Gomez says after peering into the folder, as if reading her statement.

I open my mouth to defend myself again, but what else can I say? I can shout that I didn't do it until I'm blue in the face, but who's to say they'll believe me? I was alone in that bank. All they have to go on is my word. Do I need a lawyer? *I'm so fucked.*

"Look." Anderson sighs. "We've been doing this for over twenty years. I know a criminal when I see one. I believe you didn't do it. The problem is, all the evidence points to you."

"Evidence?" My voice pitches with apprehension as my vision shifts frantically between them. "What evidence?"

"No alarms were triggered," Gomez begins to explain. "Which means the thieves knew exactly where they were and what to do."

"Meaning?"

"That this was most likely an inside job." Anderson pauses for a moment, allowing me time to let his words sink in. "You were at the scene of the crime. You've got all the keys and know all the codes. Your prints are on the vault door and all the keypads. You know the bank inside and out."

I throw my arms out to the side in desperation. "Because it's my job!" I try not to shout, but my frustration is growing. How do I get them to see it wasn't me?

Gomez sighs heavily. "Then there's the surveillance footage."

"That's good! That means the real thieves were caught on camera." So why are they questioning me?

"You're the only person that shows up in the footage," Anderson clarifies.

My stomach churns further and my heart is in my throat. "What?"

Gomez withdraws his phone and plays a video for me. It's surveillance footage of the bank. It shows me and one male who's masked and always keeps his face turned away from the cameras. We make quick work of unlocking the outer vault door, emptying a few safety deposit boxes, unlocking the inner vault door, and bagging up what has to be a few million in cash. Then the male grabs something heavy and smashes it against my head, sending me falling to the ground as he grabs the loot and bolts from the bank.

"Oh… my… God…"

I'm speechless. How the fuck do they have footage of me? I never did any of the things in the video. It had to have been tampered with somehow.

"I think I'm going to throw up." I drop my gaze to the cold metal table before me.

"Like I said, I know a criminal when I see one." Anderson's voice turns sympathetic. "I believe you."

"But you have to give us something to go off of," Gomez finishes for his partner. "Something that can lead us to the real thief, because like we said before, all the evidence points to you."

"I can't think of anyone who'd do something like this." I keep my gaze on the table and my voice sounds miles away. "Everyone who works at the bank are good people."

Anderson and Gomez stand, drawing my attention back to them.

"We'll continue to investigate. We've got tech working on this footage to see if it was sabotaged in any way. But we do have to ask that you not leave town. In case we have more questions. You are the number one suspect at this point. You and the male we hope to identify soon. If you run, it will only prove the evidence more damning," Anderson warns me.

I don't remember leaving the police station or walking to my car. One minute I was sitting in that horrible interrogation room, and the next I was in my Challenger. What do I do? How do I get out of this? How can I prove I'm innocent? I do the only thing that pops into my head. I pull out of the parking lot and make a beeline for Red Sky Security.

Chapter 22
ADDISON

I park in front of the standalone brick building and observe four other vehicles in the parking lot. Three are various styles of motorcycles and one is a powder blue Volkswagen Beetle. Though it's nearly March and still very cold in Oklahoma, that doesn't stop people from riding their motorcycles. Bikers here merely throw on a few extra layers and brace for the chill. With a deep breath, I pull open the front door and step inside.

"Hey, Addi." Phoebe beams from behind a large receptionist desk. Her blonde hair that's highlighted with baby-blue is braided into pigtails today, and her colorful framed glasses pop against her creamy complexion.

"Hey, Phoebe." I try to match her smile, but after the morning I've had, even I can feel it's a bit shaky.

I watch as deep creases form between her brows. "Is everything ok?" Her soft voice flows through the quiet lobby, and I can hear the worry lacing it.

"I…" My words clog in my throat. I'm unable to voice the help I'm desperate for. The help I came here to ask for, because I know if the men who work here can't help me, no one can.

I must look worse than I feared because a heartbeat later, Phoebe is pushing back from her desk and crossing the lobby, her heels clacking against the hardwood floors with each step. She's dressed in a bright pink wool sweater and dark grey slacks that form perfectly around her slender frame.

"Addi, what's wrong?" Full panic sets in as she captures my hands with hers. With her heels, we're the same height, so her pale grey eyes easily bore into mine as if she'll find the answer to her question written on them.

I coach myself through a few deep, calming breaths, willing strength into my voice. "Is Einstein here?"

"Of course." She gives me a reassuring nod. "This way."

I follow her through their massive conference room and into the fully stocked armory. She heads for Einstein's office, which is tucked away in the corner. When she finds it empty, she turns toward me.

"They must still be in the gym."

She motions her head toward a set of double doors. I've only been here once before, but I've never been beyond this point. Grayson told me they have a full-sized gym in the very back, and as we enter the massive space, I find three tall men standing in the back on black mats. Two of which appear to be wrestling each other. They stop at the sound of Phoebe's heels against the floor.

"Hey, Addi," Einstein, Doc, and Fuse greet in unison, each sporting a smile.

"Hey, guys."

They must've sensed the strain in my voice, or maybe it's the rigid posture, because Doc questions, "What's wrong?"

The usual silver cross earring that hangs from his left ear is missing. Presumably due to them wrestling and didn't want to risk it getting yanked out.

"Did something happen to Sweeney?" Fuse inquires, tossing his blond braid back over his shoulder so it's out of the way. The sides of his head appear freshly shaven.

"Sweeney's fine. At least, I think he is," I reassure them before taking a deep breath and turning to Einstein. "I need your help."

"Yeah, anything." He doesn't hesitate, giving me a genuine smile that touches his deep blue eyes. "Give me five minutes to clean up, and I'll meet you in my office."

Phoebe and I wait on the black leather sofa in his office and as promised, five minutes later, Einstein, Doc, and Fuse enter the room. Each is freshly showered and now dressed in normal clothes. Einstein sits in his computer chair, Doc sits next to me on the couch, and Fuse leans back against the wall with his arms crossed over his chest.

"So, what's up? You kill someone and need the body disposed of?" Doc laughs.

Before I can think about how to put it, the words fall out of my mouth. "I'm being framed for a bank robbery."

"Hardcore." Fuse nods approvingly, and I hear Phoebe gasp quietly next to me.

Einstein's brows are pulled in close, but a small grin tugs at his lips. "I'm going to need a little more detail than that."

"Y'all know the bank Renny and I work at? And about the robbery that happened last Friday?" I spare all three men a glance and in turn, they each give me a nod. "Well, I just spent my morning in a police station being interrogated and informed that I'm their number one suspect."

Doc leans forward, resting his forearms atop his knees, and asks, "Did they tell you what evidence they have against you?"

I take a deep breath and try to recall everything. "I know the bank inside and out, which would explain how not one alarm was triggered. I was at the scene of the crime. I have all the keys and know all the codes. Also, my prints are on the vault door and all the keypads."

"All of which could easily be explained because you work there," Fuse states more to himself, as if he's thinking out loud.

I take another deep breath and grimace. "Then there's the surveillance footage."

Einstein immediately twists his chair toward his wall of monitors and begins typing away. His blood-red-painted nails fly over the keys with impressive speed.

"The footage of you getting knocked out?" Doc questions.

"Not exactly… Someone tampered with the video. It shows me robbing the bank. The detectives showed it to me."

"I've got it pulled up," Einstein says over his shoulder without looking away from his monitors.

We all move to stand behind Einstein so we can watch the footage.

"How did you get it?" I can't stop my curiosity.

"I hacked into the police database." He shrugs a shoulder, and his tone suggests I should've known better.

We're all quiet as we watch the footage. Even though I've already seen it, my stomach still churns with unease.

"Well, that looks bad," Doc states flatly.

"Thanks." I glare at him before letting out a frustrated groan. "The detectives said they believe me. They have their techs working on the footage to try and find evidence of it being tampered with."

"Their tech department is a joke," Einstein snorts. "You were right to come to me. We'll get this figured out, Addi."

I sigh in relief. "Thank you, Einstein. I don't know what I'd do without you guys."

"Spend several years in prison?" Doc offers. I punch him in the arm. "Ouch, it was a joke!" He laughs and rubs the spot I hit. He could've blocked it easily but didn't.

We're all quiet as Einstein continues to work. "Let me see if I understand correctly. When y'all aren't out protecting people, you spend your days working out and wrestling with each other?"

"Pretty much." Fuse nods. "It helps us stay in shape and keeps our fighting skills sharp."

"Can you text me the link to the gym's camera feed, Einstein? You know… for educational purposes."

All three men begin laughing and despite my shitty morning, the corner of my mouth twitches up. I turn to see a slight tint warming Phoebe's cheeks, and my smile grows a bit more. Does she watch it? I know I would if I worked here, every damn morning while I sipped my coffee. I have no shame.

Though I bet if she does, her grey eyes are solely focused on one man. One tall, raven-haired man. Though I haven't known these people for long, I picked up on the chemistry between Phoebe and Einstein. Hell, a blind man could see it, yet they don't act on their feelings because of Hunter's no interoffice dating rule.

Doc wiggles his brows mischievously. "You like to watch sweaty men touch each other?"

"Who doesn't?" I chuckle.

"Don't describe it like that." Fuse runs a hand over his reddish-brown beard and shakes his head.

"You can word it any way you want. Call it fighting, wrestling, grappling, but when you break it down, it is what it is." Doc shrugs his shoulders and holds up his hands.

"They believe it's an inside job, right?" Fuse asks, getting back to the topic at hand.

I force the image of very attractive and sweaty men wrestling together from my brain and regain focus on my shitty bad luck and the true reason I'm here.

"Yes."

"I've got the case files right here." Einstein points to a monitor off to the side.

He, Doc, and Fuse read over the witness statements, what was stolen, and all the evidence they've collected. I try as well, but it might as well be in a foreign language to me. I feel a slight weight lift off my shoulders knowing they're up to date and in my corner.

"By the looks of this, I'd bet money that someone's targeting you specifically." Fuse turns to me. "Can you think of anyone you work with who has a grudge against you for any reason? It could be as small as maybe you took their favorite parking spot one day or borrowed their stapler without asking."

"No, I told the cops the same thing. Everyone I work with are good people."

If it is an inside job, I haven't the slightest clue who could be behind it. But also, a part of me doesn't want to know. The thought that I've been working next to someone every day who's capable of robbery, assault on a woman, and pinning it on an innocent person is enough to make my skin crawl.

"You just got promoted, correct?" Phoebe adds.

"Yeah, to bank manager," I answer.

"Did anyone else apply for the position?" Einstein questions as if picking up on Phoebe's line of thinking.

I'm quiet for a moment before my eyes widen and unease settles deep in my gut. "Paul. He was upset at first, but he congratulated me. He's fine now."

"Paul Nelson?" Einstein's question draws my gaze toward him.

I find a roster pulled up on another monitor. Upon further inspection, I realize that it's a list of all MoneyFirst Bank employees. *How in the hell...*

"I don't want to know how you got that so fast, but yeah, that's him." I shake my head. "Has anyone ever told you how scary you can be?" Humor fills my voice despite the heaviness of the situation.

"We don't call him an evil genius for nothing." Doc laughs, and Fuse joins him.

Einstein's angular features are full of amusement as he turns toward us. "This might take me some time, but I'll call you the moment I have something."

My shoulders drop in relief, and I feel a bit of the weight lift from them. "I appreciate it. Truly."

"No worries. We can't let you go to prison. We'd never hear the end of Sweeney's whining," Fuse jokes and I shake my head at him.

"Also, if the cops try to question you again," Einstein pulls out his phone and types away while he talks, "don't answer anything unless Foster is present. He's the attorney for Red Sky Security. I'm texting you his contact information."

My phone dings and I remove it from my back pocket with a frown. "How did you get…" I trail off. "Never mind. Evil genius, got it." I can't help but laugh, and he gives me a bright smile. "Back to your earlier question." A thought pops into my head that has my curiosity running wild as I tuck my phone back into my pocket. "Say I were to murder someone. Would y'all really help me get rid of the body?" I arch a brow at the three men before me.

All are quiet as they spare a look at each other before turning back to me.

"You're family now, Addi. We look after our own. No matter what is needed of us." Fuse's words are cryptic, but he gives me a reassuring look.

Even though I now have so many questions about what possible skeletons lie in their closets, I couldn't be more grateful to have each of them in my life.

Einstein turns and truly gets to work. As if everything he'd already found and uncovered was child's play. I say my goodbyes and make my way back home. Grayson will be back in a few hours, and I've got so much to fill him in on. What I need right now is a stiff drink and a hot bath.

Chapter 23
SWEENEY

The last thing I wanted to do was leave Addi's side. After the robbery at the bank, I spent the weekend nursing her back to health. I think the multiple orgasms I coaxed out of her helped to speed up her recovery process. You could say I did them for her benefit, that I wanted to make her feel good. But if I'm being honest, I was being selfish.

Every finish I brought her to was for *my* pleasure. I can't get enough of her. I can never touch her enough, taste her enough. I'll never grow tired of feeling her heat constricting around my cock.

When I had to go out of town for work, even though it was only for a few days, I was miserable. I missed her every minute I was gone. I missed seeing her smile at the littlest things. I missed her smartass commentary while we watched trashy reality dating shows. I missed watching her sleeping, so content and at peace. And I missed her fucking strawberry scent.

I said it before, and I'll say it again. She's ruined me, and I wouldn't have it any other way. After being surrounded by her these last six months, I never want to know what life without her would be like.

Not every assignment we go on is dangerous. Most are rather quiet and boring. We escort people to and from events, photoshoots, film sets, vacations, political events, etc. We stand by, quiet and alert to any possible threat to their safety. Luckily, we don't have to get confrontational often. However, I do love a good fight. It gets the blood pumping in a way that's addictive. But most of the time, the only action we see is fending off the fucking parasites known as paparazzi.

This particular assignment consisted of escorting a politician's only son to a concert he begged his parents to let him attend. The kid is only seventeen, and after hounding his parents for months, they finally caved, with one condition. He had to have a bodyguard at his side the entire time.

So, there I was. Thankfully, the kids got great taste in music, and we spent the night at a metal concert listening to Slipknot. Judging from the looks of things, the boy has been sheltered most of his life due to his father's career. He opened up a little and told me he'd missed out on so much growing up. I found myself sympathetic and ended up making him a deal. If he could keep a secret, I'd let him have fun.

After shaking on it like men, he got to eat greasy takeout and try his first beer. He hated it and I smiled. We joined in on a little mosh pit chaos, and to my surprise, the kid held his own. I was impressed. He even caught the eye of a pretty little raven-haired woman who I'm positive was no older than nineteen. He got to experience his first kiss, and she even let him get to second base.

I nearly had to throw him over my shoulder to get him to leave. After we got back, the kid was on cloud nine. He told me this was a night he'd never forget and how thankful he was for me allowing him to truly have fun for once. After I made sure he was safe and secure in his hotel room, I entered my own room next door to his.

A few minutes later, I received a text from Addi that had me pumping myself in the shower and coming so hard I saw white. Such a little fucking tease. She'd sent me a picture of her playing with herself, her pink vibrator slick with her wetness and placed between those thick, sexy legs of hers. That vibrator is going to be the death of me, I swear, and because I couldn't let her get away with being a little brat, I sent her one back. Two could play that game.

The following morning, I treated the kid to an endless stack of pancakes. It's not every day that someone can eat more than me but again, he surprised me. After returning him safely to his parents, I made the trip back home and groaned with relief when I entered my house and kicked off my shoes.

Two lines form between my brows when I find the house quiet. I saw Addi's Challenger in the driveway, so I know she's home. However, no TV is on, she isn't in the kitchen, and I don't hear any noise coming from upstairs. I climb the stairs and check her room. Empty. So is her bathroom. *Where the hell is she?* Worry starts to take root in my stomach as I enter my bedroom and hear a noise coming from my bathroom.

The bathroom door is wide open, but the lights are off. Candlelight dances across the walls and as I near the doorframe, I spot Addi, soaking in a bath with a glass of wine. My gaze drops to find the bottle nearby for easy refills. I cross my arms and lean against the doorframe, thoroughly enjoying the view.

Her eyes are closed, and her body is submerged, minus her head and the tops of her full breasts. My cock begins to harden at the wonderful sight before me. My bathtub is the only one with jets, and she's got them going, creating her own hot tub.

She takes a sip of her wine and releases a breathy sigh that has my now fully hard erection twitching and straining against the zipper of my jeans, begging to be set free to play. I clear my throat, finally alerting her to my presence.

She lets out a frightened yelp and her eyes fly open, landing right on me. "Don't do that! You scared the shit out of me!"

I push off the doorframe and begin to peel the clothes from my body. I love the way her vision tracks every movement I make. I can feel her heated gaze as if it were a physical touch, roaming over every square inch of my six-foot-three, bulky frame. When I'm fully naked, I step over the edge of the tub and slide down behind her, pulling her back flush against my chest.

She settles against me as I grab the wine bottle, take a sip, and set it back down on the bathroom floor.

"I missed you." I bury my nose in the hollow of her neck and inhale, breathing in fresh strawberries.

"I missed you too." She turns her head and places a kiss on my smooth cheek. I turn and capture her lips with mine.

"How was your day?" I ask as I pull back.

Addi releases a long breath, and that worry from earlier begins to sprout leaves within my stomach. "Pretty shitty."

I trace idle circles across her stomach in hopes of relaxing her. "What happened?"

What she told me next, I was not expecting. She informs me of where she spent her morning. How the cops questioned her and the latest updates on the robbery case. Then she told me she went to Red Sky Security and asked Einstein for help.

Pride and admiration replace the worry within. The fact that she's comfortable enough to recruit the help of my brothers means the world to me. I know those men had quickly accepted her, just like they did with Serenity. And it makes me smile knowing they want to help and would do anything to protect her. I'd do the same for any one of their significant others. If they had one.

I know that Einstein has this under control. I have full confidence that the evil genius will have this sorted out and solved within a matter of days. The fact that someone is personally targeting Addi makes me want to see the blood on the outside of their bodies.

I place a gentle kiss atop her head. "It's all going to be ok, sweetheart."

"I just can't seem to catch a break. When it rains, it really fucking pours." She sighs. "I'd be careful if I were you. My bad luck could be contagious."

"Then we can suffer together." I laugh before taking the wine glass from her hand and setting it aside next to the bottle.

"Hey, I was drinking that." She sticks out her bottom lip in the most adorable of pouts.

I lean in and suck it between my teeth, biting down ever so slightly and gaining a small moan from her. In one swift motion, I scoop her into my arms and stand, water falling off us and landing back into the bath.

"What are you doing?" she squeals and wraps her arms around my neck.

"You'll see." I smile wickedly and shoot her a wink as I step out of the tub and carry her into my room. I toss her atop my bed, uncaring about the water. It'll dry. "Stay," I command before turning and disappearing into my closet.

When I return, I smile at finding her right where I left her. Her eyes track me as I round the side of the bed and point to the pillows. Without question, she scoots further up the mattress.

"Good girl." She blushes at my praise. "Now, lie back."

She does and I make quick work of lifting an arm above her head and securing her wrist to the headboard with a black silk necktie. Her chocolate vision never leaves me as I round the other side of the bed and do the same with her other arm, securing that wrist with a red silk necktie. Without warning, I leave the room.

"Hey! Where are you going?" Her voice follows me down the hall as I enter her room in search of a specific object.

After a few seconds, I find it buried in the bottom drawer of her dresser. When I return to my room, I observe her trying to free herself of her restraints.

"Don't waste your energy, sweetheart. Houdini couldn't get out of those if he tried."

Her eyes shoot to mine, then to her vibrator in my hand. "What are you doing with Bob?" Her question is breathy as her chest rises and falls quickly with anticipation.

"I'm going to fuck you with it." I don't miss the way her toes curl into the covers, and a devilish grin crosses my face. "Did you think there wouldn't be a punishment for sending me a sexy picture while I was out of town?"

"I…"

Her next words die in her mouth as I climb onto the bed and kneel at her side. I press the power button and the pink vibrator roars to life. Her bottom lip disappears between her teeth, and she tracks it with her gaze as I place the tip against the column of her neck.

She gasps at the sensation as I slowly begin to drag it down the length of her body. Down over her collarbone and the swell of her breast. She moans as I circle her nipple a few times before moving to the other one, loving the way they pebble at her arousal. Then I drag it down the middle of her belly, over her pierced navel, and stop right above her sex.

"Are you wet for me?" My voice is low and hungry.

"Always," she pants, her eyes pleading with me to move it further south.

I oblige and her back arches off the bed as she moans loudly. I focus on her clit, applying a bit of pressure and rotating the head, sending her arching further and her pleasure growing louder.

"Grayson." My name is breathy as it escapes her parted lips. "Please."

I cock my head to the side. "Please what, sweetheart?"

My dick is throbbing at this point, beads of pre-cum glistening on my swollen head. Pleasuring her and watching her come undone at my actions, my touch, is enough to make me spill across her beautiful tits.

"I need… more," she pants, and her eyes lock with mine.

I grin and dip the vibrator between her legs. Sure enough, the tip is now coated with her arousal. She parts her legs further for me. An invitation that I graciously accept. Inch by agonizing inch, I slide the toy further into her core, and I don't stop until my hand hits her entrance. A cry of pure pleasure fills the room as she arches again, pushing her tits further in the air.

I graciously accept that invitation as well and bring my mouth down atop the mound closest to me. As I begin to fuck her with her vibrating toy, I clamp my teeth around her pebbled nipple. Her cry of pain turns into a loud moan as I swirl the sting away with my tongue.

With this combination, it's not long at all before she's coming. My name is a beautiful symphony as it escapes from her lips. When she comes down from her high, I straighten and remove the toy from inside her. It's coated in her juices, and I run my hand down it, gathering the wetness into my free palm and using it as lube as I grip my aching cock in my fist and begin tugging slowly.

I don't give her a warning before I reinsert the vibrator into her drenched entrance. Another cry of pleasure bounces off my bedroom walls from how overly sensitive she is right now, but I know she can easily give me another orgasm before we're done. Addi's heated chocolate gaze watches me intently. Her tongue darts out, wetting her lips, and fuck, if that's not the hottest thing I've seen.

"Do you know what I pictured in the shower last night? What I've pictured almost every night in the shower for the last six months?"

She opens her mouth to speak but finds herself unable to form words. The ego boost goes straight to my aching dick. Instead, she shakes her head no.

"You," I confess, still fucking her with her toy and jerking myself off. "I've pictured doing the dirtiest things to you. With you. I've thought about how tight that little pussy of yours would grip me. I've thought about how those full, perky tits of yours would bounce with each thrust I drive into you. About how warm your mouth would feel as you choke around my dick."

By the look in her eyes and the sounds leaving her mouth, I know she's close to coming again, and I'm right there too.

"And now I get to see how exquisite you'll look painted in my cum."

With that, we come together. Our cries of pleasure echo through my bedroom as I spill across her stomach and chest, the warm white liquid popping against her skin. I could look at her like this all day, covered in my seed. When we come back down, I finally withdraw the vibrator, turn it off, and bring it to my mouth. Again, her eyes follow every movement as I lick it clean of her multiple orgasms, loving the tangy taste of her on my tongue.

I finally untie her from my bed and carry her back to the bath. The jets were left on, keeping the water warm as we sink into the heat and wash up before going to bed, both fully sated and relaxed.

Chapter 24

ADDISON

"Hello?" I answer my phone after the third ring.

Grayson pauses the TV and resumes rubbing my feet. We've been curled up on the couch most of the day watching a *Fast & Furious* marathon.

"Hey, it's Einstein. Can you come to my office? I've got some news about the robbery."

I sit up straight. "Yes, of course. We'll be right there." I hang up and glance over at Grayson, who's got his brows furrowed. "It's Einstein. He wants us to meet him in his office."

"Okay." He stands and heads for the door, slipping on his shoes and grabbing his keys.

I follow closely behind him, and twenty minutes later, we pull into Red Sky Security's parking lot and enter the building. We greet Phoebe and make our way to Einstein's office. Fuse, Doc, and Hunter take up the couch, and Einstein sits in his black gaming chair.

"What did you find?" I skip the pleasantries, wanting to get right to business.

"Watch this," Einstein instructs and plays a video he's got pulled up on a large monitor.

It's the security footage of the bank, but instead of me in the video, it's a man I don't recognize. The video plays out, showing the man who always keeps his face turned from the camera slowly creeping up behind me and hitting me on the back of the head. I grimace and a phantom pain aches from that spot.

"I'd like to whack that little shit in the head and see how he likes it," I mutter and hear all five men chuckle.

The video goes on to show the two men robbing the place and leaving. Einstein fast forwards it a bit until it shows Serenity, Hunter, and Grayson entering the bank and finding me.

"This is the original footage," Einstein explains. "Whoever doctored the video, I give them props. They've got some talent, and it took me a bit to undo their handiwork. In layman's terms, they used a software that put your body and face over the actual person in the video, making it appear as if you were actually there, entirely erasing their presence."

"I don't recognize the guy." I try to study his face again, the true face of the robber.

I can't tell you how much of a relief it is to not see myself in that footage anymore.

"That's Donald Groger. He's been wanted by the FBI for nearly five years. He's a serial bank robber. My guess is he's got contacts that doctored the footage to frame you," Einstein explains.

"Who's the other guy? The one who always keeps his face turned from the cameras?" Grayson inquires from beside me.

"Is it Paul?" My face scrunches, unsure if I want to know the truth or not.

"Yes. I got his height and weight from his driver's license, and using a recognition software I created, that man matches Paul's dimensions. I tracked his phone and his movements since the day you got the promotion. He met with Donald at a café where they discussed the idea of robbing the bank. On the day of the robbery, he was at work all day, then his location was moved to a spot around the corner as he waited for the rest of the employees to leave. He knew that with your new responsibilities, you'd still be at the bank closing up. So, he and Donald returned, knocked you out, and robbed the place."

"Do you have hard evidence to confirm all this?" Grayson inquires.

Einstein arches a dark brow. The movement voiced a silent *did you honestly just ask that?*

"What?" Grayson holds up his hand defensively. "I just want to know if my girlfriend's going to prison or not. If so, I'll need to see about scheduling daily conjugal visits."

I send my elbow into his rib and don't miss all the men snickering from the couch.

"I've got it all right here." Einstein stands and holds up a little black flash drive. "Phone locations, conversations, images, the real footage. Everything that will prove your innocence."

He extends the drive to me, and I can't stop my hand from shaking as I accept it. My freedom. This little piece of plastic is the key to my freedom, my entire future. The pure relief I feel at this moment nearly makes me burst out in tears, but I refrain. I slip the flash drive into my pocket and throw my arms around Einstein.

I feel him tense as if he's unsure of what to do. Then he relaxes and I feel a single arm wrap around my waist as he returns the hug and chuckles softly.

I pull back and place a kiss against his soft, creamy cheek. "Thank you. You're the best!" I release my hold on him and step back to Grayson's side.

"All in a day's work, Addi." He shoots me a blue-eyed wink.

"Now, get down to the station and give that to the detectives before you lose it." Hunter stands from the couch.

"Oh, come on! Please, don't jinx me like that!"

My shoulders drop at the reminder of my horrible bad luck streak. I think I would honestly die if I got to the station only to find I've lost the only thing that will keep me free.

"You know, it's insulting that you think I don't keep backups, Bossman," Einstein comments with a sly grin.

"We've learned to never assume anything when it comes to you, Einstein." Doc chuckles.

After leaving Red Sky Security, Grayson drove us straight to the police station. The female uniformed officer at the front desk said she would deliver the flash drive to the detectives, but I wasn't taking any chances. I wanted to personally place it in either Anderson's or Gomez's hand.

After being taken back and told to wait in an interrogation room for almost ten minutes, both detectives entered. I explained everything and handed over the drive. Well, almost everything. I wasn't about to throw Einstein under the bus. I told them that I had a tech friend who looked into the case for me and gathered all the evidence. They said they'd review everything and give me a call tomorrow. And they did exactly that.

"You're a free woman again, huh?" Grayson teases as he sets a dinner plate in front of me.

I inhale deeply and my mouth begins to water from the homemade lasagna he cooked. No, I did not help him. Yes, I sat right here on this barstool and watched him while I sipped on a glass of wine. A rather large glass. I'll never get tired of looking at this man. His sheer intimidating size and ruggedly handsome good looks. Those whisky eyes of his and all those defined muscles. That sleeve of colorful tattoos that I have, on more than one occasion, traced with my tongue. I love the way his goofy personality blends perfectly with his dominating side.

"I was never not a free woman." I chuckle and shake my head as I take a bite and groan at the rich explosion of flavor.

Gomez had called earlier to inform me that Paul had been arrested and his half of the money recovered. He had tried to plead his innocence, but once the authorities found three million in cash, Paul found that hard to explain and ended up making a full confession.

He felt he should've gotten the manager position. He staged the robbery to prove my incompetence as a bank manager and to get me fired so he'd be able to get the promotion he felt was rightfully his.

On top of all that, Einstein also left the cops a very detailed map of where to find Donald Groger. Within hours, the FBI had raided the place he was holding up at and recovered the other half of the money, as well as other stolen bills and valuables from previous robberies.

The moment Gomez said I was officially free and the case was closed, will forever be etched into my brain. The stress, worry, and fear I was carrying around vanished, and I felt so light I swore I could fly if I tried.

"I'm a little upset now." Grayson grins wickedly from the stool beside me, and I smack his arm. "I was looking forward to those conjugal visits. You would've looked ravishing in prison orange."

I take another bite and wash it down with my sweet red wine. "I swear, one day, your cooking's going to make me fat."

"As long as it all goes to that round ass and those thick thighs of yours."

"You're impossible." I chuckle.

"Now that that's behind you, what's your plan?" He brings his fork to his mouth, and I can't help but track the movement. I love that mouth of his, talented in many wicked ways.

I shrug. "Go back to work now that the bank's reopened."

Grayson fidgets atop the barstool, as if nervous about something. "And do you plan to finally move your things into my room?"

I hold his gaze and square my shoulders. "No."

"What?" He nearly chokes on his food and snaps his head towards me, pinning me with an intense honey-colored gaze. "Why not?"

I raise my brow and pin him with a look of my own. "Because you haven't formally asked me to move into your room now that we're together."

Wings flutter through my stomach from my words. Together. We're together. Had you asked me six months ago if I saw myself here one day, I would've laughed in your face. I was so hurt and destroyed mentally and emotionally that a relationship or even the possibility of one anywhere in my future had me terrified. But I've come a long way since then, with the help of a wonderful man.

Our relationship went from roommates to best friends, to lovers, and now we're dating. When I think about the future now, I'm less terrified because I know I won't face it alone. I know I'll have my best friend at my side.

"My apologies, ma'am." Grayson places his hand over his heart and bows his head toward me. I can't help but roll my eyes and smile. "Would you do me the honor of moving into my room and sharing my bed with me?"

I hum and cock my head toward him. "Do I get half the closet too?"

He begins to grin. "You can have the whole fucking thing if you want."

I grip my chin and tilt my head toward the ceiling, pretending to consider my answer. After making him sweat for a few seconds, I speak. "You've got yourself a deal."

His hands cup my face, and his lips claim mine in a passionate and hungry kiss. Our mouths part and our tongues begin to taste and explore each other. I'm left breathless with a slight ache pulsing between my legs when he finally pulls back.

"Good, because you didn't really have a choice." He beams, the sight nearly making my heart stop as he turns and resumes eating his dinner.

I laugh and take another bite. "Oh, we need to go to the store soon. Your stash needs to be replenished. I kind of ate most of it. You know," I grimace, "stress eating."

His head snaps toward me, and his vision narrows. "You found my snack stash?"

I bite back a laugh. "Yes."

"And you ate it?" His tone drops an octave.

"Uh, huh." I cover my mouth with my hand to hide the smile that so desperately wants to show.

His vision drops down my frame before he brings it back up, slowly. "Hmm." His golden eyes study me.

"What?" The heat of his gaze ignites a fire in my core.

"Just trying to figure out how to punish you." Again, his vision drops down my front. "I could tie you up and use Bob on you again." My pulse begins to quicken at the reminder of how amazing he made me feel the last time. "Or… Or I could watch a few episodes of the new season of *Love Is Blind* without you."

I genuinely gasp and glare at him. "You wouldn't dare!"

He shrugs his shoulders, twists forward again, and resumes eating like he didn't just threaten to TV cheat on me.

"I love you." The words slip out before I realize what I've just confessed.

I thought I'd never say those words to another man again. Not after what Jack put me through. But I don't regret saying them. I've felt this way about Grayson for a little while now. The love started as friends and then grew into something beautiful, unrushed, and completely unexpected. I just didn't know how to say them. Or if I wanted to be the first one to voice them.

"I know." He grins wickedly at me.

"Did you… Did you just quote *Star Wars* to me? The very first time that I voice those three *very important* words?" I don't know whether to be mad or impressed.

"Sure did." He wiggles his thick brows mischievously at me, and all I can do is smile and shake my head. "I love you too, sweetheart."

"From the first day?" My question is a whisper as emotions clog my throat.

He leans in and places a soft kiss against my cheek. "From the very first fucking day, baby."

And somehow, from hearing those words come from his lips, the last pieces of my broken heart are put back into place. A heart Grayson spent months helping me mend. A task I thought impossible and couldn't be happier to be proven wrong. I, without a shadow of a doubt, know that we're going to make it. That we'll have a wonderful, long, and happy life together.

My palms become clammy, and my nerves are all over the place. I've been up shit creek without a paddle quite a few times in my day and in fights where death was a high possibility, but this… What I'm about to do has me more nervous than I've ever been before. I pat the pocket of my slacks for what has to be the dozenth time as I wait for Addi to join me. As if the object that's hidden within will magically disappear if I don't check on it often.

I wait for Addi in the foyer of our Airbnb beach house we rented for a small weekend getaway in the Florida Keys. My weight shifts from foot to foot until I hear the stairs creak, and my gaze shifts up. The sight before me has my heart skipping a beat like I'm a damn teenager admiring the most popular and beautiful girl in school.

She's dressed in the same little blue sundress she wore the day we met all those months ago. I specifically requested she pack the outfit, loving the way it hugs her curves and shows off those thick legs and the tops of her full breasts I love so much.

Her makeup is done, causing her chocolate gaze to pop against her tan skin, and her brown and blonde hair falls down her back in luscious waterfall waves. When she reaches the bottom of the stairs, she slips on her sandals, and I don't miss the way her vision drinks in the sight of me. I absolutely love the way she looks at me, with such love, admiration, and of course, a hunger that I'll never get enough of.

"You look fucking stunning, sweetheart." My voice is thick with desire.

I'm half tempted to carry her back upstairs and ravish her for hours, but there will be time for that later. I've got important plans for us tonight that I've been setting up for weeks now with the help of Serenity. She gives me a bright smile, and a small blush paints her cheeks at my compliment.

"And you look devilishly handsome." She gives me a wink as we leave and climb into our rental car.

It takes us twenty minutes to get to the little beachside restaurant that overlooks the water. We choose a table outside so we can enjoy the afternoon weather and the gentle sea breeze. Even after a wonderful meal with great food and light conversation, I'm no less nervous. This is one thing in life I've never done before. One thing I never foresaw myself doing, but the moment I met Addi, everything changed. If I'm being honest, as the minutes pass, my nerves grow and tighten the large knot in my stomach.

After dinner, we head back to the beach house, ditch our shoes, grab a blanket, and spread it out atop the warm white sand. The sun is setting, painting the sky in stunning hues of pink and orange. I have an arm draped around her shoulder as Addi snuggles further into my side. I place a kiss atop her head and breathe in her soothing scent of strawberries, allowing it to calm me for what's to come.

"This has been a wonderful trip." She sighs contentedly. "Thank you for planning it. It was nice to get away from work for a few days."

"It has been amazing." I know she can hear the smile in my voice. "I'm half tempted to buy this place, so we never have to leave."

"That would be wonderful." Her full, honest laugh pulls at my heartstrings. "Though I'd miss our family and friends."

"I can't believe Big Daddy and Renny are engaged now. I thought I'd never see the day he'd settle down."

Boss and Serenity had taken a vacation a few months back to a cabin tucked away in the mountains, where they got snowed in for the whole weekend. He'd proposed to her, and she'd said yes. I couldn't be happier for my brother, and when he asked me to be his best man, I grinned like a complete idiot. He constantly denies it, but I knew I was his favorite.

"I know!" She beams. "I can't wait to help her plan the whole thing. It's going to be magical." She sighs dreamily.

Serenity had asked Addi to be her maid of honor. It's only fitting since the two are as close as sisters.

"I agree, but I think ours will be better."

Here it goes. I've steered the conversation onto the topic at hand, and as long as I can get my damn nerves under control and not fumble over my words like a lovestruck idiot, this should go smoothly. She pulls away so she can peer up at me.

"Our wedding?" A look of surprise shapes her rounded features. "That's a little presumptuous of you."

I cup her chin and peer into her chocolate gaze. "It's confidence, sweetheart." I give her a cocky grin.

Her mouth parts slightly, and my vision drops to her full lips. Her chest rises and falls quicker as her pulse kicks up, and the vision goes straight to my groin. I claim her lips and stand, pulling her hand with me, causing her to stand as well. Then I remove the small box that's been burning a hole in my pocket all night and drop to one knee.

She gasps and her breath quickens further. "Grayson, what are you doing?"

"Addison." I hold her hand and peer up at her. Emotions clog my throat as I observe the goddess standing before me, her hair and dress gently blowing in the breeze, the sunset coloring the sky behind her. "You stole my heart the day we met like a thief in the night. I thought I was content with the way my life was, but then you walked in and wrecked my world in the best way possible. Now, I can't picture the way my life used to be before you, and I don't want to. After loving you, I never want to experience what life would be like without you. You are the very air I breathe and without you…"

I can't even finish the thought as my mind goes back to that day in the woods nearly a year ago when those thugs had her pinned to the forest floor. I was close to losing her, and I never want to feel that pain, that desperation, that fear ever again. I clear my throat and forge ahead.

"You've become my best friend, my lover, my girlfriend. It would make me the happiest fucking man in this galaxy if you'd do me the honor of becoming my wife. Will you marry me?"

I release her hand and open the black velvet box. Though we've known each other for almost a year, we've only been dating for a handful of months. But that doesn't matter. I knew she was the one I wanted to marry the day we met.

Addi isn't one of those girls who loves big, flashy jewelry. If she did, I would've bought her the biggest damned diamond I could find. Her tastes are simpler. So, with the help of an overly joyous Serenity, I found her the perfect ring. A simple silver band with a small purple stone in the shape of a heart that's surrounded by tiny glittering diamonds. She gasps for a second time as her hands come up to cover her mouth. I know, by the look in her eyes, I picked the perfect ring.

"I know you might have some hesitation about marriage, given your past, but I don't care if we're engaged for three or even ten years before you're ready to marry. These words and this ring are my promise to you that I'm here to stay. That I love you and will always love you."

"Grayson, it's beautiful." The tears that filled her vision during my speech now cascade down her cheeks. "Of course I'll marry you!"

I pull the ring from the box, slip it onto her ring finger and stand. She throws her arms around my neck and crashes her lips against mine. I grip her ass and hoist her up as she wraps her legs around my waist. Though I knew she would say yes, the relief that floods through me at hearing the confirmation from her lips is euphoric.

I pull back and we're both panting. "Good! Because if you said no, I would've had to tie you up in our bedroom until you changed your mind."

She sucks her bottom lip between her teeth at my sinful threat. "You can still tie me up when we get home." Her words are sensual and now my erection is pulsing painfully against the zipper of my slacks.

I lower us onto the blanket, where she's flat on her back, and I'm nestled between her warm parted thighs. "Such a dirty girl." I grin wickedly as I nip at her neck and lick the sting away.

She arches her chest into me and moans. I made sure to find a house so secluded from society that we wouldn't ever be bothered by neighbors or other tourists. With the entire beach to ourselves, I feel her reach between us as she fumbles to undo the button and zipper of my slacks. I help her push them down far enough to free my aching erection that's beading with pre-cum. My hand snakes beneath that glorious dress of hers and freezes.

I raise my brow. "No panties?"

"No." She gives me a wicked smile.

"Fuck, sweetheart," I growl as I align the head of my dick at her soaked entrance. "You're going to be the death of me."

With a hard thrust, I bury myself deep inside of her heat. I groan and she gasps as we become one in the most primal way. And, with the entire beach to ourselves and my ring resting snugly on her finger, we make love, right there, beneath the setting sun.

Don't Miss Out

Here's a sneak peek at the final book in the Desire Series.

Desire's End

Chapter 1

The house alarm chimed three times, pulling Serenity Jinx from her TV show as her head swiveled toward the massive dark oak front door. Rays of afternoon light filtered through numerous windows, flooding the open-concept main floor with natural light. Her vision softened when they landed on a familiar figure.

Hunter walked through, locking it behind him as he kicked off his boots and crossed the spacious living room. The simple crimson T-shirt and blue jeans he wore framed his tall stature, accentuating his sculpted muscles and broad shoulders. A physique that could only be achieved after years of rigorous military training, sending her bottom lip disappearing between her teeth at the sight of her fiancé.

"Hey, Angel." He kissed her on the lips as he laid stomach down on the couch, wrapped his arms around her waist, and nestled his head in her lap.

Warmth ignited within her chest, as it always did whenever he was near. Though his woodsy-scented cologne had dimmed throughout the day, faint hints clung to the fibers of his clothes as if refusing to drift away with the passing breeze. She didn't bother stopping herself as she took a long, slow inhale.

Home. That was what home smelled like to her. It didn't matter where in the world they were, what structure sheltered them, or who they were with. As long as this man was by her side, she was happy.

"Hey, sweetie. How was work?" she asked as she removed the elastic tie from his hair, letting his shoulder-length brown strands fall loose as she began to massage her fingers against his scalp.

A groan of pleasure slipped past his full lips as his ice-blue and hazel eyes slowly drifted closed. "Long." He released a heavy breath. "Send me behind enemy lines with nothing but a rock and I'd be like a kid in a candy shop, but paperwork…" He groaned again. "I hate paperwork. How was your day?"

Hunter Gatlin was a former Navy SEAL, but after leaving the service, he founded his own security company. Red Sky Security provided short-term bodyguard services for affluent clients for a variety of occasions. She knew that since he didn't have protection duty today, he was in the office most of the time, responding to emails and sorting out paperwork, invoices, and things of that nature.

She couldn't help but laugh. She knew better than anyone that her fiancé wasn't the kind of man who could sit behind a desk for hours each day. He'd go stir crazy two days in. Thankfully, she knew that Phoebe Vega, his receptionist, tended to handle the bulk of the paperwork for him, which he compensated graciously with a healthy salary for all her hard work. But some things were beyond Phoebe's control, requiring the owner's attention.

"It was good. Addi and I did some shopping and had lunch. We mostly discussed wedding plans."

A part of her had feared planning both her and Addi's wedding at the same time would get crazy, but it's been surprisingly fun. Addi was her best friend. They'd met five years ago at the bank they still work at and grew as close as sisters. Last year, Serenity found herself in need of a new date for Addi's first wedding after she found her long-term boyfriend, Noah, in bed with another woman.

Addi had suggested using the dating site, Desire, to try a type of speed dating in hopes of finding a new date. Luck was on Serenity's side, and after a few questionable dates, she'd met Hunter. It was nearly love at first sight for them both and they'd been inseparable ever since.

Hunter burrowed his head further into Serenity's lap. "Sweeney keeps giving me shit about him being the favorite at work because out of everyone, I picked him to be my best man."

She laughed and shook her head as she kept massaging his scalp. There was no malice in his tone. She knew he loved Sweeney and all the men he worked with like brothers. "I think he'll be gloating about it for the rest of his life."

"Probably. The man has the maturity of a twelve-year-old boy."

"Ah, but you can't help but love him."

She smiled, and her mossy gaze shifted to the diamond ring that now adorned the finger on her left hand. Her mind transported her to the past. To a day she'd never forget, even if she lived to be a hundred. A few months back, Hunter had surprised her with a spontaneous trip to the mountains, where they got snowed in at a beautiful cabin. He'd proposed, and they spent the rest of the weekend in a mess of tangled limbs in front of a roaring fireplace.

"Oh, I checked the mail earlier and there was a letter from Desire," she said, snapping back to the present.

Serenity reached over and picked up the rectangular, cream-colored envelope that rested on the end table next to the couch, handing it to him as he propped himself up on his elbows.

"Really?" he questioned as he removed and unfolded the piece of paper. "What do they want?"

Dear Mr. Gatlin and Ms. Jinx,

We at Desire love to see success stories like the ones both of you experienced while using our dating site. It is our mission to help as many people find the other halves of their souls as we can. As a gift, we've chosen a handful of couples who've had success just like you two. We want to celebrate you all with an all-expenses-paid vacation to our island resort in the Bahamas for a week of relaxation and fun. If you have any questions, please, don't hesitate to reach out. We hope to hear from you soon and to see you there.

Sincerely,

Patrick Grundy – Marketing Director

He remained quiet as she watched his vision move over the letter again, slower this time.

"Sounds like a scam." He snorted and passed the paper back to her.

"Don't be so pessimistic." She slapped his shoulder lightly as she shook her head incredulously. "It could be real."

Companies entice new and existing customers with trips as marketing tactics all the time. Hell, the bank she worked at just did something similar last year, allowing anyone who opened a savings account with them to be entered for a chance to win a three-day cruise for two to Mexico.

"I don't know, something seems off."

"You have to admit, it does sound amazing." She couldn't stop the sigh of joy that escaped her parted lips. "I'd kill for a vacation to a tropical island."

Though Hunter frequently traveled around the world for work, she couldn't tag along for numerous reasons. All of which she completely understood. However, that meant that the only trips she got to take were few and far between, when they both could get away from work for a few days.

"Have you forgotten what happened the last time we vacationed on an island, Angel?" He arched his thick, scarred brow at her.

She knew he was referring to what had happened at Addi's wedding last year. Hunter was even more of a saving grace after Addi and Serenity found themselves kidnapped by Jack, Addi's ex-husband. Apparently, he'd been infatuated with Serenity and was only with Addi to get close to her.

Jack had orchestrated an off-the-wall plan that sounded like an insane plot for a thriller movie. He was a criminal defense attorney and, after observing his client's mistakes and taking notes, had formulated what he thought was an airtight plan that would allow him to get away with murder.

He'd taken a huge life insurance policy out on Addi and hired a couple of criminals to murder her the day after their wedding so he could collect the money and live the rest of his life with Serenity in a large home he'd bought in Hawaii.

After both women were kidnapped by Jack, Hunter and Sweeney came to their rescue and brought them home safely. Several months went by as Addi and Sweeney's relationship blossomed from roommates to best friends, then to lovers when he helped her heal over the loss and betrayal Jack had put her through.

"That was different," she tried to protest, but sounded doubtful herself.

His deep chuckle filled the quiet room around them. "Was it?"

Serenity opened her mouth but closed it again, unsure of how to respond. She hated it when he spoke rationally. Sound logic wasn't what she wanted right then. She wanted a beach vacation surrounded by sun, sand, and all the umbrella drinks she could get her hands on. Her face contorted into a pout and she felt her shoulders deflate.

A languid sigh slipped past his lips, and she knew he hated to see her with anything but a smile on her face. "I'll have Einstein look into this for us. If it's real, we can talk about it more."

That instantly perked up her spirit.

"Really?" She beamed.

She knew he'd never tell her no. He responded with a slight nod before resting his head back down on her lap. She resumed the massage of his scalp, nearly putting him to sleep as she continued her TV show.

The following morning, Hunter pulled his blacked-out Harley Sportster into the parking lot of Red Sky Security. A single-story, standalone brick building with bulletproof windows lining the front. Two crotch rocket motorcycles, one black and green, the other black and red, and a powder-blue Volkswagen Beetle were parked out front. After resting his bike on the kickstand, he stood and entered through the front door.

It was unlocked. Phoebe was usually the first one here in the mornings, unless Einstein pulled an all-nighter, but none of his men were on any dangerous assignments at the moment, so Einstein's constant monitoring wasn't needed.

"Good morning, Boss." Phoebe gave him a beaming smile, her colorful-framed glasses popping against her creamy skin.

"Good morning, Blue," he greeted back with a smile that would most likely never be as bright as hers.

That's the kind of woman Phoebe Vega was. Heart of gold, soft-spoken, always happy. She'd worked for him for nearly three years now, and she was the glue that held all the men together around there, though they'd never told her that. Not that it was some big secret, but rather because they weren't the kind of men who openly shared their feelings like that.

The first receptionist he'd hired put more effort into trying to sleep with them all than doing her job. It was a nightmare. He'd given her multiple warnings, but she never listened, which resulted in him firing her. Phoebe walked into the conference room for an interview to fill the position, and after one look at her, he knew she was the right person for the job. Thanks to his previous profession in the military, he'd always been a good judge of character.

Phoebe had never once crossed the line with any of them, and she quickly became a little sister they all looked out for and would kill for. Since she was a member of their family, it was only fitting that she had her own nickname. Blue, because of her hair—long, light blonde strands with baby-blue highlights throughout.

He walked down the hallway lined with all their offices, entering the last on the left. After placing his helmet and keys atop his desk, he made his way back into the open and airy lobby, through a set of double doors that led to a conference room with a massive table and enough chairs to seat twenty comfortably. He kept walking through another set of double doors that led to the fully stocked armory and a room tucked away on the right-hand side.

That was Einstein's office. Hunter had tried many times to offer the guy an office next to all of theirs, but he kept refusing, saying he liked his privacy. Which was understandable. Hunter was the same way, but that didn't stop him from keeping an office by theirs empty in case Einstein ever changed his mind.

With a quick glance, he found the room empty and knew the men must be in the gym. He kept walking back, passing through one last door that led to a fully stocked gym equipped with cardio machines, circuit machines, and a massive free-weight section. In the back of all that, the concrete floor was covered with black mats. That was where they grappled and practiced fighting each other to keep their skills honed and sharp, in case they were ever needed while on an assignment.

If they had a meeting with a client, they would show up to work dressed in a nice shirt, slacks, and dress shoes to help look the part. To show they can look professional but still protect at a moment's notice. If they didn't have any meetings, they arrived in workout clothes and hit the gym. Then they'd spend at least an hour or two sparring with each other, and once they were done, everyone was free to leave for the day.

Hunter had four really good guys who worked under him. Each was given their own call sign that was unique to them. Doc was a skilled sniper and gun enthusiast, named after the infamous gunslinger, Doc Holliday. Fuse was an explosive expert and pyro enthusiast. Sweeney preferred knives over guns, so he was named after the fictional serial killer from the mid-1800s, Sweeney Todd, who killed people with straight razors. And Einstein was the brains of their operations—a computer genius, skilled hacker, and avid gamer.

As suspected, Hunter found Einstein and Sweeney had already started on their workouts. Einstein was in the middle of a rep of squats and Sweeney was using the bench press to work out his chest. Fuse was on an assignment and Doc had left for a week-long vacation. After a quick greeting to the guys, Hunter slipped in his headphones, turned on his music, and lost himself in a killer back and bicep workout. By the time everyone was done, they were layered in sweat.

They took to the mats and began sparring, first Hunter and Einstein, then Einstein and Sweeney, and last, Hunter and Sweeney. Though Einstein never went out on assignments, he still worked out with everyone and somehow had one of the best ground games Hunter had ever seen. The kid was tall, lean, and lightning-quick, making wrestling with him a good challenge and always fun. Everyone called him a kid, but only because he was the youngest amongst their family at twenty-three. Well, besides Phoebe, who was the same age.

After everyone was exhausted and dripping sweat come lunchtime, they hit the locker room, showered, and changed into casual clothes. After bidding goodbye to Sweeney, Hunter followed Einstein into his cyber cave.

A large, wooden L-shaped desk filled the left side of the space. Numerous monitors of various sizes were mounted on the wall above. A large flat-screen TV was mounted on the opposite wall with a sofa positioned in front of it. Einstein, clad in his usual style—a dark hoodie, jeans, and a beanie—pulled out his black gaming chair and sat down.

"You mentioned you'd found something?" Hunter inquired.

"Yeah, Bossman, I looked into the letter you sent me, and from what I can tell, it's legit." Einstein turned to face him.

His shaggy black hair stuck out like wings beneath the worn gray beanie, his deep blue eyes popped against his pale skin, which was free from any tattoos or piercings, and he always had his fingernails painted. Today, they were dark blue.

Hunter was given the call sign Boss. Though the explanation is self-explanatory. However, each man had a different variation of the name. Einstein always called him Bossman, Doc and Fuse addressed him as Boss, and Sweeney, the adult-sized child, referred to him as Big Daddy.

"The company, Desire, owns an island in the Bahamas. They purchased it almost a year ago and started construction on the resort immediately. Patrick Grundy, the guy who signed the letter, *is* a real human being and is Desire's marketing director. They've sent out the same letter to three other couples across the country. One couple is from Rhode Island, another is from Georgia, and the last is from Washington. They also sent one to a woman, however, hers was an apology letter, offering the same week-long vacation. I remember seeing the story in the news last year.

Apparently, this woman had met a man on the site who turned out to be a stalker and kidnapped her. He was a real creep, and she put him six feet under."

"Good for her," Hunter responded.

He knew all too well the damage a stalker could inflict on a woman. Jack had stalked Serenity in the weeks leading up to his wedding to Addi. Serenity was a wreck about the whole thing, to say the least. But he was glad that whoever this woman was, she was strong enough to end her stalker. That's one less sicko in this world and this planet is better off because of it.

"Well, Angel will be happy that the offer's real." He couldn't help but laugh lightly, knowing his fiancée would want to start packing, even though it was a few weeks away.

He'd asked how Serenity felt about it, but how did *he* feel about the whole thing? He was skeptical at first, thinking it was some elaborate hoax, but after Einstein's research, he believed in the legitimacy of it. He'd believe just about anything the evil genius told him. The kid always seemed to know way too much for his own good.

Do we go? Do we stay? A vacation did sound pretty good to him. Though he traveled around the world a lot for work, he rarely did it for pleasure. The last vacation he took was months ago, when he proposed to Serenity. A memory tugged one side of his lips up. The look of shock across her angular features when he'd popped the question, the love that filled her mossy eyes, the way her body felt beneath him after she said yes and they made love.

However, that was months ago. They were well overdue for a vacation, just the two of them, filled with relaxation, fun, and sex.

Lots of sex. *Damnit*, he sighed to himself. Just like that, he'd talked himself into it.

"Thanks, man. I appreciate it."

"Anytime, Bossman." Einstein smiled and twisted back toward his monitors.

Hunter watched as Einstein clicked a few buttons on his keyboard, and one of the large screens changed to what looked like a video game. A man dressed in a blue and yellow jumpsuit appeared to be exploring a decrepit town many years after an apocalypse. Hunter shook his head and chuckled to himself. Although he'd told Einstein numerous times not to play video games while at work, none of his men were currently on dangerous assignments, so he often let it slide.

For My Readers

Thank you for reading A Healing Love. I hope you enjoyed Grayson (Sweeney) and Addi's love story as much as I did. I would love to hear your thoughts about it, so please leave a review and follow me on social media to stay up to date on my latest writings.

Facebook: Maricca Wood - Author
Instagram: mariccawoodauthor
TikTok: mariccawoodauthor
Website: www.mariccawood.com
Newsletter: www.mariccawood.com/newsletter

Acknowledgments

First and foremost, the utmost praise goes to my Heavenly Father. Without Him, none of these works of art would be possible. Though we all face various struggles throughout life, some casting true depths of sorrow and despair upon us, remember Psalm 23:4. "Even though I walk through the valley of the shadow of death, I will fear no evil, for you are with me; your rod and your staff, they comfort me."

To my husband—I've given you a shout out in every book so far, and I'll continue to do so. Without your love, patience, and unwavering support, my books would never have left the privacy of my computer.

To my mother—I will forever be grateful for the plotting sessions we had while floating around your pool listening to great music! Together, we came up with some pretty juicy stuff. And thank you for always picking up the phone and chatting with me for hours as you helped to smooth out any plot holes I stumbled across.

To my Beta readers—Y'all are incredible! Without your trusted input, this book may have fallen flat.

To my editor, The Havoc Archives—Once again, your skills polished this book to be the best version of itself possible. You're a rock star!

To my cover designer, Books and Moods—Y'all outdid yourselves on this one. I fell in love the very moment I saw the cover.

To my readers—Without your support, none of this would be possible. All I want to do is share love stories with the world and like-minded people who'll appreciate them as I do. I'm grateful to each and every one of you guys.

Maricca Wood is a hopeless romantic who, believe it or not, used to loathe reading growing up. Now, she finds it hard to put books down. She writes contemporary romance, some darker than others, and fantasy, all with plenty of angst, relatable characters, and of course, spice!

She lives in Oklahoma with her family and possesses an associate degree in Entrepreneurship. She enjoys reading a wide range of genres, playing video games, watching anime, doing puzzles, and building Lego sets. She can count on one hand all the people who have ever pronounced her name correctly the first time. Good luck!